MW00895759

the invisible Polly McDoodle

Mary Woodbury

Sir Alexander Mackenzie School
61 Sir Winston Churchill Ave.
St. Albert AB
T8N 0G5

COTEAU BOOKS
WWW.COTEAUBOOKS.COM

With thanks to my son Robert who doodled in sixth grade, Cathy Gravelle who checked the court and legal data, the fourth graders in Hillview School, Edmonton, who listened to the second draft, Peter Carver who edited so well, and of course, my husband Clair, who types better than I do and is far more patient.

© Mary Woodbury, 1994. Fourth Printing, 2001.

All rights reserved. No part of this book covered by the copyrights hereon may be reproduced or used in any form or by any means—graphic, electronic, or mechanical—without the prior written permission of the publisher. Any request for photocopying, recording, taping, or storage in information storage and retrieval systems of any part of this book shall be directed in writing to CanCopy, 1 Yonge St, Suite 1900, Toronto, Ontario, M5E 1E5.

This novel is a work of fiction. Names, characters, places, and incidents either are the product of the author's imagination or are used fictitiously. Any resemblance to actual persons, living or dead, is coincidental.

Edited by Peter Carver
Cover painting, oil on canvas, 1994, by Janet Wilson.
Cover and book design by Duncan Campbell.
Typeset by Karen Steadman.
Printed and bound in Canada by AGMV Marquis.

Canadian Cataloguing in Publication Data

Mary Woodbury, 1935-
The invisible Polly McDoodle
ISBN 1-55050-062-7

1. Title.

PS8595.064415 1994   jC813'.54   C94-920165-0

COTEAU BOOKS
401-2206 Dewdney Ave.
Regina, Saskatchewan
Canada   S4R 1H3

AVAILABLE IN THE US FROM
General Distrubution Services
4500 Witmer Industrial Estates
Niagara Falls, NY, 14305-1386

The publisher gratefully acknowledges the financial assistance of the Saskatchewan Arts Board, the Canada Council for the Arts, the Government of Canada through the Book Publishing Industry Development Program (BPIDP), and the City of Regina Arts Commission, for its publishing program.

contents

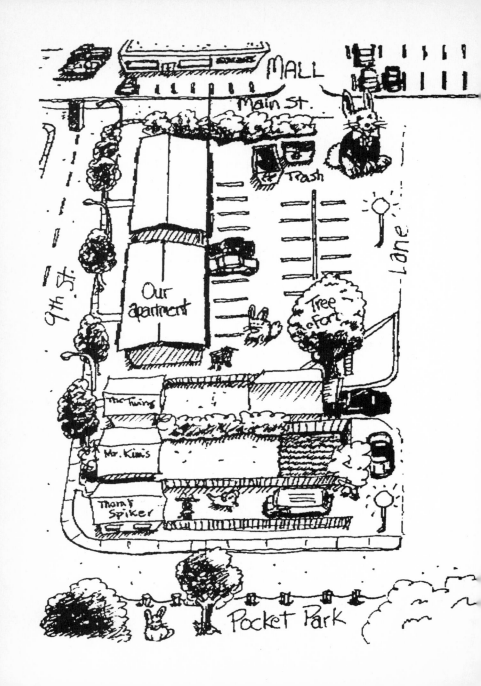

1. The Elusive Rabbit Appears

"POLLY McDOUGALL, YOU'D LOSE YOUR HEAD IF IT wasn't tacked on," Polly's dad laughed when he heard she had left her new lime-green ski jacket on the bus. "Is this what Christmas week is going to be like?"

Polly stared down at her worn pink sneakers, ears burning. Her dad, Ted, turned his attention back to slicing carrots into the stew bubbling on the stove. The steam rising from the pot fogged his glasses. He hummed "Good King Wenceslas."

"You'll have to phone." Polly's mom sat at the kitchen table flipping pages of the phone directory, looking for the number of the city bus lost-and-found. "Last week you left library books on a park bench, and the week before it was sneakers at the Y." Reddish-blond strands of hair fell across Jan McDougall's forehead and she swept them back with an air of impatience.

"She just wants attention, that's all." Polly's big brother kicked off his big boots in the vestibule of the apartment. Shawn pushed past Polly into the kitchen and stood in front of the open refrigerator surveying the contents with a frown on his face. "There's nothing to eat."

Polly wished a trapdoor would open in the grey nubby carpet beneath her feet so she could disappear, all four feet of skinny girl with bruises on her knees and red hair that fell in her eyes. Some days being a kid was hard. Was it her fault if so much stuff was going on at school that she couldn't keep her mind on what she was doing? She'd taken her coat off because it was too hot on the bus. Then she and her friend Robin had nearly missed their stop, so they'd dashed for the door. She'd remembered her keys, her sketch book, and her knapsack. So she wasn't all bad, just half. The Half-responsible Polly McDoodle sighed.

"Hey, kid, I'm sorry I teased you, okay?" Her dad rubbed his five o'clock shadow on Polly's cheek. "I had a tough day, too. Had to let one salesclerk go because he hid from the customers in the back room. And some jerk walked off with a pair of our top flight basketball shoes from the stand at the front of the store." Polly's dad massaged the back of his head, like he was trying to push the worries out through his salt and pepper curls. His big brown eyes blinked several times. The lines at the corners of his mouth and between his eyebrows wrinkled.

"You should get out of retail," Polly's mother said. She was drawing up the chart for next week's chores and menus. She kept the whole house organized, just like she did the Y. Polly figured her mom would organize the whole country if she was given the chance.

"Save some stew." Polly's dad pulled a bright sports coat over sturdy arms and a barrel chest. "Can't keep Excelsports waiting."

"I went on a tour of Kirby Junior High today," Polly said, speaking for the first time since the storm over her lost jacket had started.

"Only artsy wimps go to Kirby, small fry." Shawn hoisted his hockey bag over his shoulder. "Two more practices before the big game." He caught up to his dad at the apartment door. Father and son looked alike, except Shawn's hair was pitch black and he was three inches taller than his dad. "Is everyone coming Thursday night to watch?"

"Wouldn't miss it for anything." Both parents laughed at speaking at the same time.

"Might be scouts from the majors," Polly's mom added. The three larger McDougalls filled the apartment with loud, excited voices as they said their goodbyes. Polly's dad and Shawn flew down the stairs, thumping and bumping. The door crashed below. Polly bit her lip and spoke quietly.

"Kirby has three art rooms and a drama class." Her words dropped into the suddenly silent room.

In the kitchen Polly's mom scooped potato, carrot, and onion peelings from the cutting board and threw them in the white plastic garbage bag under the sink. She rinsed her hands under the tap, ran them along the sides of her bright lilac winter jogging suit and did up her fancy runners.

Polly stared at the top of her mom's head. "Kyle's going to Kirby," she said, louder.

"Let's get Christmas over with, honey. We've got enough to contend with with Shawn's game, special cooking, gifts to buy, parties at work." Polly's mom lifted anxious eyes. "You're young yet. It's much too early to be thinking of your future. You'd be better concentrating on remembering your belongings. We just bought that jacket. Money doesn't grow on trees, you know."

Her mom stretched both arms out to the wall, bent and limbered her calf muscles. "Give the stew a stir in a few minutes, will you?" She was out the door and down the hall before Polly could answer.

Polly's ears burned. She knew she'd upset her mom and it made her feel bad. She stood by the window in the silent living room, soaking in the peace, trying to calm down.

Traffic hummed on Ninth Street, and a siren wailed near the Royal Alex Hospital. The street lights came on all at once, creating pools of yellow light around each tar-stained lamp post. Christmas lights strung on balconies flashed on and off. Green, red, and blue bulbs outlining the rooftops blinked and gleamed. The darkness seemed friendlier with the glow and sparkle of lights. It was less than a week until Christmas, and she was the Excited Polly McDoodle.

Car headlights lit up the parking lot revealing the dilapidated tree fort in the old willow tree where she and Kyle Clay (otherwise known as "the Clam") and Robin Weinstein hung out whenever possible. Polly shook her head in surprise. Sitting at the base of the tree, bolt upright, eyes shining pink in the glaring light, a giant hare shivered in its white coat of fur. Only the rabbit's ears and feet were brown to match the frozen brown grass.

"Your camouflage isn't working, you poor rabbit. If there was snow we couldn't see you. It's a good thing you don't have many enemies." Polly opened the patio door, stepped into the cold air and stared down the lane past the cars in the parking lot. No snow, just brown grass, black bare trees, grey asphalt, and frozen black gumbo in the empty back gardens. A little snowfall would bring magic to the landscape.

She would love to draw a picture filled with snow and Christmas trees and kids on sleds. Drawing was the next best thing to breathing, Polly figured. She loved the smell of pencils and art erasers, paints and charcoal. She loved taking a blank piece of paper and filling it with colours and shapes. She knew she wasn't a great artist yet, but she would be some day. Her fingers itched to pick up her sketch pad.

She stirred the stew instead. Then she picked up the phone and put it back down. She did that three times, trying to get the nerve to call about her jacket, call the number Mom had circled in the directory. She felt dumb. This year at school, even at home, it was important not to look dumb.

Her voice quavered as she asked for her jacket. The woman left her hanging on the receiver listening to "Frosty the Snowman." While Polly waited she doodled a chain of rabbits across the top of the page.

"It's just come in." The lady interrupted the next song, cutting poor Rudolph off just as he was laughed at by his friends for having a shiny nose. Polly didn't have a shiny nose, but her family made fun of her doodles. None of them could draw. Her dad hummed "Polly Wolly Doodle All The Day" every time he saw her with a sketch book.

She promised the woman she'd pick up the jacket the next day, Tuesday, after school. She'd ask Robin to go with her.

When her mother came back from her run, she did her stretches, showered, and joined Polly for supper.

"Thursday's the school concert." Polly reached for her milk.

"Uh-huh."

"I'm singing in the chorus."

Polly's mom buttered her wholegrain bread neatly, spreading a tiny dab of fat-free margarine over the whole slice. "I thought you didn't have a part this year."

"We all sing in the chorus. Kyle's playing a solo."

Her mother lifted a forkful of stew to her mouth. "It's Shawn's big game, you know. Polly, sometimes I think you think up things to say to make our life complicated. Didn't I just tell you that what with the game, work, cooking, and gift buying we had enough on our plates? I don't want to hear about the concert."

"I painted the backdrops."

"Can't we see them some other day?"

Polly was busy mashing her potatoes, shoving her carrots to the side of the plate. She hated food all mixed together – she liked to keep everything separate. Besides, Polly liked her carrots raw, like rabbits did.

"Polly, I'm talking to you," her mother said sharply. "School concerts bore me. They're all the same."

"So are hockey games," Polly pressed the tines of her fork into the potatoes harder.

"How can you say that? Your brother is one of the best Junior hockey players in the whole city. He's got real potential. We might produce a famous McDougall yet."

"He's a dumb jock." Polly's face blazed. A lump of meat lodged in her throat. She choked.

Her mother banged her back. "That's what you get

for having a fit of jealousy. Your day will come, young lady. Wait until you're older and become really good at something."

Polly blushed and bent over her dinner. She took a bite of potatoes, but they were cold and soggy like wallpaper paste after all that mashing. Her mom was grouchy again and she didn't know why. Recently it had been like she, Polly McDougall, couldn't do anything right. She didn't remember her mom getting mad at her so often when she was a little kid. Now, almost daily, it seemed, her voice got sharp and her face turned red. Polly shook her head, trying to clear her thoughts.

She nursed her milk, tipping the glass this way and watching it coat the sides with white, then drain away. It made interesting shapes, like hills and valleys, and rolling countryside, whiter than rabbits, whiter than city snow.

Polly glanced at her mother's face with its big, blue eyes, a smattering of freckles, long lashes, dimples, and flowing wavy hair, tied neatly when she left for work at the Y. Her mother's muscles rippled like a dancer's. She'd been in ballet and modern dance for years. Polly was small, like a stick with elbows and knees. She knew she had the grace of an elephant. She didn't move well like her mom or her dad did. He'd played hockey in the minors until his knees gave out. Maybe the McDougalls picked up the wrong baby at the hospital and some really klutzy family had a graceful ballerina or gymnast for a kid. Maybe the Real Polly McDoodle was Polly Sprints or Double-jointed Dolly.

"Stop your everlasting dreaming, Polly. It's time you walked George. Isabel said something about running over to the mall," Mom said.

Polly had a job this winter walking the neighbour's wire-haired fox terrier every night. Isabel Ashton was afraid of falling on the ice or having the dog pull her arm out of its socket, she said. Besides, she and Polly had something in common. Isabel was an artist.

Polly hunched over, ignoring her cold dinner, and doodled a rabbit on the back of her hand in ballpoint.

"Earth to Polly. Earth to Polly." Mom waved a soggy tea towel in front of her face. "Walk the dog."

Polly covered her hand so her mom wouldn't see the doodle and yell at her again. Her mom was afraid of blood poisoning or something. Tattooing was fun. Maybe Polly could join the circus – what a great career that would be! The Totally Tattooed Polly.

Tucking a pencil and pen into her pocket along with her keys, Polly snuck into the corridor. The invisible, invincible Polly McDoodle crept along the wall, ready to pounce on intruders or aliens. The smell of curried chicken floated from 202. Overhead in 303, Kyle Clay was practising scales. By the time Polly reached 204, Isabel Ashton's door, Kyle had switched to the piece he was playing at the concert Thursday night.

Polly stood before Isabel's door and slid her hand slowly down the white wall towards the doorknob.

George snorted and woofed. His sharp nails scratched the inside of the door. So much for Polly, the invisible stalker of terrible foes. That dog could hear a hat drop. Isabel claimed that George would give thieves, hoods, and hooligans real trouble. They'd drown in tongue lickings. Polly shuddered, her imagination inventing black-jacketed hooligans in the apartment hallway. She'd watched both a mystery and a cop show on TV last night. Maybe the Famous Polly McD. should be a detective, like the woman in the latest series.

"Is that you, Polly?" Isabel called from her studio as Polly opened the door. George jumped up and licked her fingers and chin, cleaning off the last of the stew. He pranced along beside Polly as she made her way down the hallway. What a dumb mutt. Polly grinned and tickled the dog under his chin. He moaned with delight. A flicker of matching happiness filled Polly's chest as she bounced into the studio.

"Glad to see you. Going to the mall. Need some last-minute presents for the nieces." Isabel's sentences were shorter than George's leash and clipped closer than his winter haircut.

Isabel stood before her latest canvas. She was wearing a wide wool plaid skirt, a bulky yellow sweater and an old shirt over top. Pink-tinted bifocals rested on her nose and cheeks. Her eyes sparkled. A tad of yellow paint was smeared on her forehead close to the curly white hair. The room smelt of turpentine, oil paints, and coffee.

Polly joined Isabel. The easel held a wide prairie landscape with a ripening canola crop and a startling blue, cloudless sky. Wild roses scrambled up the crumbled corner of a broken-down log barn. The brush strokes were bold, the colours bright. The painting was nearly finished.

"It's so bright."

"Warms my winter mood."

"I like it." Polly wanted to reach out and touch the canola field...but she didn't. "I'm not that bold."

"You will be."

George woofed, stood on his hind legs and put his

paws on Polly's arm.

"Just a minute, you old mutt." She pushed him down. Isabel said it took a lot of determination and courage to be an artist...that and practice, practice, practice. A picture of herself as the Talented Polly McDoodle grew in the corner of her mind. She was wearing one of her dad's cast-off shirts, painting a picture in a bright studio.

Isabel interrupted Polly's dream. "What about your picture? Need more time?"

She and Polly walked together to the table under the window. Polly took the watercolour she was working on, the one Isabel had helped her get just right, out of its protective art folder. Her parents' Christmas present was nearly finished: a rendering of a log cabin her folks had spotted by Pigeon Lake last summer, one Shawn had taken a photo of, one her folks had oohed and aahed over all the way back to Edmonton. Polly couldn't buy the cabin for them, but she could draw it. She slipped it back in the folder with a sigh.

"They can't come to the concert on Thursday. Shawn's game."

"Will one retired school teacher sitting there be any solace?" Isabel wrapped one wide arm around Polly's skinny shoulders. The warmth of the hug passed through Polly's body like an electric current. Isabel continued, "I love school concerts. First year without one in forty years. Retirement isn't easy. I miss the kids. Besides, I want to see those backdrops of yours."

"Did you always want to be an artist, Isabel?" Polly asked. George groaned, gave up on his walk, and rested his curly snout on his paws.

2. A Box of Memories

ISABEL WALKED OVER TO THE WHITE STORAGE CHEST and pulled out an ancient leather art portfolio. She laid aside a stained cedar box with the initials "I.A." burned on the top. Isabel slid out a pile of grubby pieces of art work.

"My folks were farmers, practical, hardworking folk, no time for tomfoolery." She lined up her early work across the back of the table. "Mom saved these, though. Best artist in the 4H Club, four years running. Here's my County Fair ribbons."

Polly pored over the pictures and shiny ribbons with gold print. Farm animals and buildings, fruit bowls and flowering trees, a wooden bread board, cheese, and a half loaf of crunchy farm bread, a jug of cider.

"These are great," Polly grinned. "What's in the box? Paints, chalk, charcoal?" She lifted the dusty wooden box in both hands. "Can I see?"

The room grew silent. Polly lifted her eyes and searched Isabel's face. The hazel eyes had misted over, the smile had disappeared. Polly felt a cold draft from somewhere. She lowered the box back onto the table. Had she done something stupid again?

"Wait a minute, Polly." Isabel's wide hand rested on Polly's sleeve. "It's all right. Open the box."

Polly hesitated, as if opening the box would be invading Isabel's life.

"It's the last gift my fiancé Harry sent me, before his ship sailed from Halifax in 1943. The convoy was attacked. His battleship was torpedoed. There were no survivors." Isabel sighed. "That's war for you." Her usual brisk voice was so low and slow, it didn't even sound like Isabel. Polly wished she had never touched the box.

"I'll just walk the dog — okay?" Polly picked up the leash and the pooper scooper and backed toward the door.

Isabel held up her hand. Polly stopped. Then Isabel pulled the box toward her. She unhooked the brass hasp, her large hands gentle as a grandmother's holding a new baby. Colour returned to her cheeks. Polly's fingers itched to sketch Isabel bending that way over the box, the planes of her face thawing, her eyes clearing. Polly felt energy and excitement flowing in the room again. Ever since the retired art teacher had moved in last summer, Polly and Isabel had been friends. She loved visiting Isabel's quiet suite, maybe because of George, or the art — or maybe because here was a grownup who wasn't in a hurry, who had time to talk to a kid who seemed to spend half her life feeling stupid.

Polly's heart skipped a beat as the lid was lifted. She was overtaken by a lingering feeling of fear mixed with a sense of wonder. Her mouth was dry as dust. What an imagination, Polly McDoodle. How could anything precious as what Isabel was about to show her bring any danger with it? Did Isabel's sadness weigh so much?

Isabel removed a layer of creamy satin and revealed the contents of the box.

She smiled. "I haven't dared look at them. Too many memories," she sighed. "But it's fine. I'm fine. They are beautiful, aren't they? It's a shame to keep them hidden away like that."

Four rows of rainbow-coloured gems nestled in little grooves on a bed of cream satin. The brilliance of the polished stones dazzled Polly and the brightness of the blue velvet drawstring bag fastened to the underside of the lid made her blink. What a feast! Polly felt suddenly as if she knew what it would be like to discover hidden treasure. She loved the colours so much her eyes hurt.

Isabel pulled two tarnished chains from the bag, one gold and the other silver. She took Silvo and a soft rag from the shelf and handed Polly the silver chain to shine.

"Harry found them in a pawn shop in Halifax. Said I was his rainbow girl. Said I was a gem." Isabel rubbed the gold chain until it gleamed in the palm of her hand. She stared out the window into the dark night. "I couldn't stand the sight of them, not after the telegram came saying he was missing in action. He was dead. I made a life without him. World War II cast a long shadow. I have memories, though."

Polly laid the shiny silver chain on the creamy satin liner. So much of people's lives were hidden, like icebergs. Her teacher said the ice you see on the top of the ocean is only a fraction of the floe. That's why the famous ship, the *Titanic*, had sunk; it struck a giant iceberg. Isabel had a giant iceberg inside her, a big cold, sad part, and dumb old Polly McDoodle had run smack dab into it. What a day.

"I better walk the dog, Isabel." Polly reached for the leash. George sprang to his feet.

"Garnet for fidelity. Amethyst for sincerity. Carnelian for comfort. Bloodstone for courage..." Isabel picked up each one, caressed it and put it back in its groove, the small silver or gold eyelet facing the top of the box.

"The carnelian is pretty." Polly couldn't pull herself away from the beauty captured in the box of jewels.

"Would you like to try it on?" Isabel whispered.

"I couldn't."

She pointed to the next one in the row – a red and green stone cut in the shape of an animal. "What's that?"

Isabel picked it up and peered at it. "If I'm not mistaken, that's a heliotrope. According to my grandmother, a heliotrope could keep the wearer invisible."

Wow! Wouldn't that be neat. Imagine having a stone that would let you hide when life got too much, when you lost stuff or felt stupid.

Isabel threaded the heliotrope onto the silver chain. "Here, my girl, just what you need." She dropped it over Polly's short reddish curls. "Now you can be the Invisible Polly McDoodle."

Polly reached up and pulled the little stone away from her chest so she could stare at it. "It's a rabbit, too. That's great, rabbits are my favourite. I saw the giant hare sitting beside our tree tonight just before dinner." She felt the warm smooth stone between her finger and thumb.

Isabel closed the box and left it on the work-table.

George woofed in disgust. Polly clipped on his leash and they both trotted towards the door.

"Lock the door when you bring George back. I'm off to the mall. Might stay for coffee and a cinnamon bun."

Polly reached under her bulky jacket and her blouse, and once again touched the heliotrope bobbing on her bony chest. It clanked against the apartment keys, so she took her key chain off and pushed it into her pocket. She didn't want the heliotrope scratched.

Running down the back steps she nearly collided with Arturo, the new kid in 403. He had a *Journal* bag slung over his shoulder. He was small, dark-haired, dark-skinned, and wiry, and something about his brown eyes made Polly nervous. George licked Arturo's hand. Arturo dug a cookie from his pocket and gave it to George. The boy nodded his head at Polly and scurried away. Talk about icebergs. Arturo had a whole raft of them inside.

Polly chewed her lip. Her dad had reminded her yesterday that she and Kyle and Robin should make friends with Arturo DeCosta and his little sister Rosalie. After all, they were refugees. They came from a country where they weren't safe. She wanted to make friends, but Arturo played soccer with the boys in the school yard. He didn't hang out around the apartment building. Kyle should talk to him, but Kyle didn't talk much, to anyone. Besides you can't just walk up to a kid and say, hi, we're neighbours, let's be friends. Especially when he kept his distance, almost like he was afraid of them. Polly kept hoping something would happen to make getting to know him easy.

Outside in the clear, crisp night air, Polly's breath

made fog. George pulled her down the laneway at top speed towards the pocket park between the elementary school and the junior high. He trotted along, proud as a thoroughbred horse, tight curly grey and black hair with floppy brown ears and a short curved tail. As they reached the park Polly undid his leash and let him run. He sniffed dead grass clumps, watered trees, and did his business. Polly put it in the trash barrel. "If it wasn't for Shawn's stupid allergies, I'd have a dog like you, George. You're a good boy."

The fox terrier nuzzled her knees. Wind blew across the park, carrying the smells of car exhaust from Ninth, and cabbage cooking from some house on the laneway. Less than a week until Christmas and still no snow.

George tugged like a sled dog from the Arctic as they walked back down the lane behind the houses on Polly's block. The German shepherd chained by Rudy's Body Shop snarled and leaped at the gate. "Beware the Dog," one sign said. "Private Property. Keep out," a red sign said underneath. There were no Christmas lights, no lawn ornaments, and the windows were covered with blinds and old blankets. Polly shivered. That place had always given her the creeps. She'd never stopped there, not once – not even for Halloween or to sell raffle tickets.

The springer spaniel behind the punk pair's house stared glumly through the slats in the broken picket fence. A motorcycle and a beat-up van were parked by the decrepit garage. Loud heavy metal music blared. Polly and Kyle had watched the two punks move in last fall. A gang of bikers had helped them carry their stuff into the house. The girl Polly thought of as "Spiker" didn't look much older than the senior high kids lounging around the mall.

George lunged for the black cat perched on the Kims's cedar fence. The cat darted away. George tore the leash out of Polly's hand and took off after the cat, Polly racing after him, hollering. The Kims had lived there quiet as mice ever since Polly could remember. They handed out homemade taffy apples each Hallowe'en. Their front garden had hundreds of geraniums and marigolds all summer and fall. The mountain ash in front of the picture window held tight little clusters of bright red berries all year round. Small birds chattered there and the Kims's cat sat wistfully beneath the tree's branches.

A wide beam of light snapped on overhead. Polly blinked in the glare. Kyle the Clam hung over the railing of the tree fort, sweeping his flashlight over her face and down the lane. George watered the willow tree and sat on his haunches, waiting for Polly.

"What're you doing?" Polly wrapped George's leash around a post by the nearest parking spot. She climbed the rope ladder, mumbled the password, and pulled back the burlap curtain.

Kyle sat on an orange crate, dressed like a polar explorer: buttoned, mittened, his parka hood tied tight. His folks worried about his health like he was still a little kid. Polly and Kyle had been buddies since kindergarten. When she was just a kid, she had heard her mom and dad talking one night about the Clays being a funny couple to be parents, having a baby late in life, and then the kid being so slow to talk that the school had tested him, thinking he was a slow learner. Turned out Kyle went off the IQ charts the other way. He was smarter than all of them. He just didn't like to talk. Polly had always kept an eye out for him. She'd beaten the second grade bully for teasing Kyle about never talking. She could still remember the blood on her T-shirt, first bright red and then drying to a brown rust that never washed out.

Kyle clutched his newest dungeons and dragons book and his bag of dice and weird creatures. Every time he bought new pieces he'd show them to Polly without saying a word, just smiling to himself. Kyle leaned over his metal trunk, unlocked it, and threw them in.

"Let me guess." Polly sat on an upturned wooden box. "Your folks have decided D. and D. is bad for your health." Kyle nodded.

Polly spotted one of Kyle's twelve-sided dice as it rolled across the floor and fell through a crack. She got down on her hands and knees and reached through the hole.

"Shine the light down, will you?" As she reached through the hole the heliotrope rabbit swung out in the flashlight beam. Her hand closed on the dice and she hauled it up gingerly. She heard a clunka-clunka, looked around, but couldn't see anything out of place.

Kyle was staring at the stone on the silver chain around her neck. He took the rescued dice and shut it in his metal trunk, uncapped a black marker from his pocket and scrawled "Do Not Touch!" on the lid.

"It's a heliotrope, supposed to make the wearer invisible. Isabel lent it to me." Polly said. "It's a lucky rabbit. I saw the giant hare who lives in the park, sitting under the tree, right here in the parking lot."

George moaned. Kyle scrabbled in his pocket. Cellophane crinkled. The mighty polar explorer threw a handful of sunflower seeds to the dog, then handed Polly a fistful.

"Whenever your folks act like that, you shut up like the real clam you are, you dumb kid." Polly punched Kyle's padded chest. "I didn't do anything. We're friends, aren't we? You can talk to me, can't you? I need to talk to you. I've been thinking we should change the name of the tree fort. Shawn heard us calling it 'HideAway' when he left for practice last night. Remember? Robin stood shouting the password at us as he walked by."

Kyle said nothing.

"Besides 'HideAway' is boring. We should change it to – to something exciting – something exotic." Polly blushed. She liked the sound of that word, exotic.

"What?" Kyle asked in a hoarse whisper, as if his voice was rusty.

"The house of the heliotrope, or the invisible hare, or something."

The two of them sat on boxes for a couple of minutes. Kyle kicked the base of one branch with the toe of his sneaker.

"Did you try to explain?" Polly asked.

Kyle shook his head. Then he heaved a big sigh and opened his mouth. "Dad gave a thirty-minute lecture on the long-term negative effects of war games, violence, terror, and misrepresentation of prehistoric animals and medieval myths. It didn't seem worth it."

"At least you've got the tree fort," Polly sighed. "What about 'The House of the Invisible Rabbit'?"

"He's not invisible. We've both seen him."

"Wears a camouflage."

"He's elusive, that's what the rabbit is, not invisible." Kyle perked up. "We could call it 'The House of the Elusive Rabbit,' and to be a member you have to have seen him."

"It could be a her." Polly rubbed the heliotrope between thumb and finger. "It could be a girl like me, like Polly McDoodle. Elusive. I'd like that."

George barked. "I have to take him in." Polly waved as she backed down the rope-ladder leaving Kyle sitting there, pale eyes, pale face, a wisp of straw-coloured hair peeking out from under the hood of his jacket. "You look like Scott of the Antarctic. Don't stay out 'til you freeze, idiot." A crazy picture of Kyle and her as Famous Arctic Explorers popped into Polly's mind. Polly had done a social studies project on Scott just last month. She giggled, thinking about she and Kyle doing anything so brave. Between thinking of icebergs and arctic explorers, she must have cold on the brain.

A motor roared in the laneway. The next-door neighbour, a small guy who looked like Danny DeVito, pulled his gigantic old white Lincoln into the garage. The friendly giant, his roommate, who drove a red MG, appeared at the back door.

"What are the Twins up to?" Kyle appeared with his flashlight at the top of the ladder.

"Looks like the small one bought the big one some flowers. Maybe a Christmas poinsettia."

"Either that, or it's a marijuana plant and we've got crooks." Kyle's laugh sounded like an extended sneeze. "They're always carting plants in and out."

Polly unhooked George and made for the door. Mr. Beamish, the bearded guy from 101, was coming out. He held the door for her and bowed like a gallant knight. They both grinned.

In Isabel's Polly emptied George's water bowl, rinsed it, and let the tap run until the water was icy-cold. Meanwhile she doodled on a big writing pad that lay on the counter by the kitchen phone. She drew her favourite picture, a giant rabbit with a coat and a vest and bow tie. She even took time to shade in his haunches, put a cloud in the sky. She thought briefly of doodling Polly and Kyle as Intrepid Arctic Explorers but instead filled George's bowl with cold water and put it on the floor. She leaned the picture of the rabbit up against the sugar bowl where Isabel would be sure to see it when she got back from the mall. Then she tiptoed out of the apartment, leaving the dog lapping fresh water. She pushed in the doorknob quietly, pulling the door closed without a sound. There, it was locked. Isabel's phone rang. Polly could hear it. Too late, she couldn't answer it. The door was locked.

Isabel probably meant she should deadbolt it. Polly reached for the key chain around her neck. She touched the heliotrope but no keys. She felt in her jacket pocket and her jeans pocket. The keys were gone. That was impossible: she remembered putting them in her pocket.

Where were the keys? Where had she been? Polly retraced her steps in her head: she'd put the keys in her pocket in Isabel's before she had gone to the park – lane – park – lane – tree fort – Isabel's. Had she left them on the counter beside her sketch of the Elusive Rabbit? A well of panic opened inside her stomach. She walked towards her place, misery mounting by the moment.

Her apartment door was open. Her mom must be doing the laundry downstairs. Polly slipped inside and threw herself down on the old maroon couch. The figures on the TV screen flickered. Polly paid no attention.

No way could she tell her folks she had mislaid her keys today, not after losing her jacket. No way.

3. A Robber In the House

FOOTSTEPS THUNDERED DOWN THE HALL. MUFFLED voices shouted. Polly dashed to the apartment door, stuck her head out.

"It's right this way, officer," a loud voice called.

"What's happened?" Polly asked. No one seemed to hear her.

Her dad and Shawn stood in the corridor talking to two uniformed police officers. Isabel and Polly's mom stood in the doorway to Isabel's apartment. Their faces were red and blotchy, and Mom had her arm around Isabel's shoulder. Red flashing lights from a police cruiser shone through the tall vestibule windows.

"What did they take?" Dad gestured wildly, like a soccer coach with an unruly team.

"What happened?" Polly asked again, louder this time. The adults paid no attention.

"Isabel's been robbed." Shawn answered. "Merry Christmas, all you campers."

The Razis from 202 stood in their doorway – mother, father, three tiny bright-eyed children in pajamas clustered around their parents' knees.

"Perhaps we could sit down," one police officer suggested. "Two detectives are on their way."

Mom led the way back to the McDougall apartment, motioning to Polly to put water on for tea and coffee. Polly could feel her chest tightening, and a lump of fear the size of a golf ball jammed her throat. She rubbed the heliotrope between her thumb and first finger.

Words and phrases drifted in from the living room. "Gem collection – radio alarm – small Christmas presents." Oh no, not the box of stones! Isabel had just gotten them out, had just showed them to Polly. Blood pounded in Polly's ears. Your fault, you stupid kid – you made her open the box, and you were the one who didn't double-lock Isabel's door.

Shawn came bursting into the kitchen and filled a tray with soft drinks. The doorbell jangled. Polly jumped.

"Boy, are you nervous!" Shawn giggled. "You aren't the criminal type. It's not your fault."

"That's what you think."

"Jeez, it could have happened to anyone. You're the worst one for feeling guilty. It's not your fault." Shawn threw up his hands in despair. "Might as well talk to a wall."

Polly took the fresh pot of coffee and a tray of mugs, milk, and sugar and followed Shawn into the front room.

Isabel was sitting on the couch between Polly's mom and dad. Her face looked greyish.

"This is Polly. She'll fill in the missing details." Isabel's voice sounded flat. Polly glanced around the room. Two uniformed police officers slurped coffee.

The two detectives sat on dining room chairs, straight-backed, polished shoes, creased blue trousers.

"I'm Sharon Mills, Polly," the short blonde detective said. Her lipstick was pale pink, her earrings small blue balls. "This is Detective Anderson." She pointed to the tall burly man with the neat flattop, balancing a note pad open on his knee. He grinned and his teeth were even and very white. "Please go over your movements from the time you and Isabel left the apartment."

Polly glanced around the room nervously. Her parents sat with their hands in their laps, their faces regarding her with encouraging smiles. Her brother Shawn was holding up the wall, leaning sturdy and innocent as a tree trunk.

"There's nothing to worry about, Polly." Her dad couldn't stand big gaps in the conversation. He leaped in with words. Sometimes Polly needed time to think. She wished she had heard Isabel's story. She wished she knew how the thieves had gotten in. Had they forced the lock, or had they a set of keys, or had they broken in the patio door? Polly's heart was hammering so hard it felt as if there was a bird caught inside her chest. Maybe they had used her keys. Maybe they had gotten through the door because she hadn't double-locked it.

The adults sat waiting. Her mom frowned. "Polly, just tell the truth. Nobody blames you. Don't be silly, child."

George barked from down the hall. He was probably lonely and scared. Polly could understand him, she could really understand him. She bit her lip.

"I took George for a walk."

"What time would that be?" Detective Mills asked.

"I don't know."

"Exact times don't matter to our Polly," Mom said. "She's a dreamer. She left the apartment about seven o'clock."

"Isabel and I talked for a while," Polly said quickly. Polly and Isabel exchanged glances. Polly didn't want to say anything about her folks' Christmas picture, their talk about dead Harry, the war, and the box of memories. That was between them.

"I left for the mall pretty soon," Isabel said. "Polly and I went out at the same time."

"Did you lock the door?" Detective Mills asked quietly. Polly and Isabel both shook their heads.

"In this building we keep an eye on one another's places." Polly's dad's voice filled the silence. "We're all friends here."

Detective Anderson cleared his throat. "The door was not forced, sir. Could be an inside job."

Polly chewed her fingernails.

"Not very smart," Detective Anderson scolded. "Robberies, break and enter, car thefts are up. It's the season, of course. But we're beginning to suspect there's a gang."

"Where did you take the dog?" Detective Mills asked. "How long were you out?" Her eyes were as blue as her earrings, her eyebrows raised in slim hoops. She smiled.

"I took George to the park. I came back." Should she tell them she stopped at the tree fort?

"Did you see anything suspicious?" Shawn asked. The policemen glared at him. He closed his mouth. "Sorry," he said.

Polly grinned. Look who looked stupid now. She relaxed a little. "I stopped at our tree fort in the back yard for a couple of minutes. Then I brought the dog in, gave him fresh water, and locked the door."

"Are you sure you locked the door?" Detective Mills asked. "Think carefully now."

"Did you throw the deadbolt?" Detective Anderson asked. He was wearing a blue tweed jacket with leather patches on the elbows. The top pocket drooped from the weight of his pens.

Polly stared at him.

"What time did you get home?" Detective Anderson asked. He shook his pen three times impatiently before he changed to another. He waited for her answer.

The room seemed too full of questions.

Her mother was watching her, frowning. "I think we have had enough questions for one night, officer. Polly is still a young child. She needs her sleep. There's been too much excitement for one day."

"I locked the door," Polly stated flatly. She did not say, "I am not a little kid," to her mom, but she wanted to. She fought back tears. "Honest, Isabel, I locked the door." Please God, don't let me cry, not here, not in front of everyone.

The police officers were leaving. Her outspoken mother had saved the day. Isabel gave Polly a big hug without saying a word.

"Isabel, did I leave my keys on your counter, beside the phone and your sketch pad?"

"I didn't see any keys. I'll look again."

Polly broke free from the hug and reached for the chain around her neck, the chain with the heliotrope rabbit. "Here, it's all you have left."

"Pshaw, child. I lent it to you. You wear it. Look kinda funny on a big woman like me." George barked down the hall. "My canine friend is lonely. I must go home. Sleep well, Polly."

Polly nodded and headed down the hall to her room. Her parents were talking and doing the dishes together. "Goodnight, honey. Sleep tight!"

How could she be expected to sleep after a day like this? The Far from Famous Polly McDoodle wouldn't sleep well, not until she had helped discover who had stolen Isabel's stuff, not until Isabel had her box of precious stones back in her wide hands. If she still believed in Santa Claus, that's what Polly would ask him for Christmas.

Instead of an easel and watercolour paper for me, she whispered to the dark and silent room, Santa dear, give Isabel back her box of memories.

4. A Code, a Map, and a Puzzle

NEXT MORNING POLLY PULLED ON HER "I LOVE THIS Planet" sweatshirt and faded jeans. She tugged the brush through her red hair, stared at herself in the mirror, made a funny face by putting her lips out like an orangutan's and giggled. She grabbed the heliotrope from the night table and dropped it over her head, tucking it under the sweatshirt. The Magnificent McDoodle was ready for another day.

"Breakfast!" her parents yelled.

Polly's mom and dad leaned against the wall in the hall, panting, doing their cool-down exercises. "It's crisp out there," Polly's dad huffed and puffed like Red Riding Hood's wolf.

Shawn appeared in his bedroom doorway, rumpled, grumpy-looking, his wavy hair covering his brown eyes. "Who invented mornings, anyway?" he grumbled and closed the door.

After gulping orange juice, cereal, and toast with mounds of grape jelly, Polly hurried to collect her things. She had to concentrate – don't forget your math, your library book, Kyle's calculator that you borrowed, she told herself in a half-whisper. She tossed them in her purple backpack, picked her lunch up from the counter and headed toward the door where she stopped to put on her old ski jacket with the short sleeves and torn pocket. Today was going to be better. The Thoroughly Efficient McDoodle whistled through her teeth.

"Have a good day, honey!" Her dad stood by the sink. Shawn's voice in the shower belted out Christmas carols off key. Polly winced.

"Have you got everything? Your keys?" Dad asked.

Polly nodded and ducked through the door and down the stairs. She had her lunch and her math, so she wasn't quite lying by not telling her dad about the missing keys.

Kyle from 302 and Robin from 304 were already in the lane. Robin had on her hot-pink ski suit with high white boots and a white sports bag. Dark curls ran riot down her back past her shoulder blades. Her face was round, and pink from the cold, with huge almond eyes hooded by long lashes, and thick eyebrows that Polly envied. Kyle was busy putting a neatly packed bag of garbage in the dumpster and washed out tins in the bright blue recycling box.

"I lost my keys," Polly said.

Kyle didn't say anything, shook his head, glanced up at Isabel's balcony, and over at the tree fort.

"I know, I should retrace my steps. We can see if they show up on the laneway." Polly jogged up and down to keep warm. "All that and a robbery, too."

"What robbery?" Robin banged her mittened hands together and moved down the lane towards the school.

"Does everything happen when I'm out?"

"I missed it too," Kyle mumbled. "Music lesson."

Polly told the whole story of the robbery with gestures, arms flung out, and pointing back towards Isabel's and towards the pocket park. Kyle, meanwhile, searched the frosty laneway for signs of Polly's lost keys.

Arturo DeCosta and his sister Rosalie came scurrying along behind the three friends.

"Did you hear about the robbery?" Robin shouted as the two new kids hurried past. Arturo turned his head away quickly and tugged his sister's hand, dragging her towards the school yard. Rudy's dog, Chief, growled as they passed.

"What's his problem?" Robin shrugged her shoulders.

Rosalie glanced over her shoulder as her brother pulled her along. "*Que paso?* What happened?"

"What happened?" Kyle spoke slowly. "What happened was a robbery. Bad people broke into Isabel Ashton's apartment."

Polly was surprised every time Kyle said more than two words. She watched as he caught up with the little kid and ruffled her shiny black hair.

The first buzzer sounded from the school. The three friends ran towards the doors. Rosalie and Arturo talked rapidly in Spanish, shouting at each other over the noise of the school yard.

"We should invite Arturo to join the tree fort," Polly whispered to Kyle as they took their jackets off. "But does he know enough English to work on codes or play games? Rosalie is pretty young. She's only in third grade." Listening to the two Latin American kids talking Spanish made Polly's head dizzy. Did hearing English all the time make Arturo's head dizzy, or make him feel stupid?

"I bet it's not easy, being in a strange country, leaving your dad behind in a dangerous place." Kyle drew air through his teeth in a low whistle. "I'll get you spare keys." Then he marched into the classroom, his mouth glued shut again.

Polly stared after him, stooped to pick up her coat that had fallen on the polished green and grey tile floor. What a funny guy! Sometimes she thought Kyle read her mind, knowing she was thinking about the DeCostas, knowing how much she was worrying about her keys.

"Polly, are you joining us?" Jonesy stood at the door of the classroom, his bristly brushcut head nearly scraping the top. He tapped his foot. Polly blushed to the roots of her red hair, then squeezed past her skinny beanpole of a teacher and made her way to her seat. The kids giggled. Too bad the heliotrope didn't work, she thought, fingering it. Now would be a good time to be The Invisible Polly McDoodle.

In the afternoon they rehearsed for the concert on Thursday evening. Polly and the other artists finished the backdrop for the big number: a map of the world with stars showing where the students or their parents came from. Polly had gold paint spattered on her cheek. Kids in the school came from forty different countries. Polly's star was in Ontario, because she had been born there, and her mom and dad – even her great-great-grandparents. She was an old Canadian. It made her feel kind of happy, kind of secure.

As she put Arturo and Rosalie's stars in their small Central American country she saw how far away from home they were. She had to figure out a way to break through to them. Tell them that they had friends, if they wanted some. No one should feel so cut off.

Robin hollered at her from the door of the art room. "Boy, are you miles away or what? I come along and you're painting and gluing on stars, and you don't even see me."

Polly dropped her brush into the paint pot. "Sorry."

"So, are we going to the bus place?"

"What bus place?" Polly brushed paint splatters off her cheek.

"Your coat, remember?" Robin said. "One lime-green ski jacket."

Polly gave her head a shake, wiped her hands on a paint rag and left the nearly finished world map. The two girls took the bus to Sir Winston Churchill Square. The downtown Christmas lights flashed and glittered, the colours so rich they seemed to give off sounds of bells and music.

"Hard to forget this, it's so bright," the woman behind the counter laughed as she handed the neon jacket across the counter.

"I'll make sure she gets it home," Robin chuckled.

Robin and Polly clambered off the bus at Ninth Street and headed down their old familiar lane, skirting a tumbled bag of garbage torn open by some loose dog, probably the punk pair's spaniel, Brutus. They let him run sometimes.

"Kyle must be in the tree fort." Robin pointed to the orange surveyor's flag tied to the bottom branch.

He was reading a paperback novel as they hauled themselves up the rope ladder.

"Elusive rabbit," they whispered. They wanted to keep their new name secret.

"All clear," Kyle said quickly. He rooted in his pocket and lifted out a new set of keys and handed them to Polly. "You owe me three bucks."

She checked them. There was the outside key, her apartment key, and Isabel's key. "How did you get these?"

Kyle shut his eyes and closed his mouth in a firm line. His giant glasses slid down his nose, past the freckles, and he pushed them up again silently with long thin fingers.

"You've got more secrets than the government." Robin punched his arm.

"I'll keep watch." Polly perched on the cedar railing where she could survey the whole laneway: parking lot and mall entrance at one end of the block, park fence and school yard at the other. She clasped the sketch book Isabel had given her for her birthday and three sharp pencils she kept in her crate in the tree house.

Kyle and Robin discussed a new code for sending notes.

"I read about this neat cipher. You use the name of some famous person like Winston Churchill, David Suzuki, or Princess Diana."

"Why not Madonna, Cher, or Kermit?" Robin laughed. "I don't know any of those other people. They must be old."

"It has to be a long name." Kyle stood up and leaned against the rickety railing. "Winston Churchill was a great leader in the Second World War. David Suzuki is a Canadian who is trying to stop us from polluting the planet. Princess Diana – well, you know her."

"Okay, okay, I'm just giving you a hard time, Kyle." Robin threw a handful of raisins at him. "Lighten up, old man."

Polly listened with one ear to her two friends and doodled in her book. Her feet dangled over the side and banged against the plywood wall. "So tell us, Kyle. How does the cipher work?" Polly was drawing a picture of the block as if she was a bird flying overhead. It was really too dark to see but she used the street lights and her memory to fill in the details.

"Say you use Winston Churchill as the key. W is A. I is B. N is C. S is D and so on." Kyle said.

Robin frowned. "What about repeats like the second I or the two Ls. There aren't enough letters in the name."

"That's part of the secret. You leave out letters in the name if they occur a second or third time. When you match as many letters as you can, start over. L is W2. M is I2. N is N2." He held up an black notebook where he'd figured it all out. Polly had been listening carefully but she didn't look up.

"Let's write a message, right now. For Polly. She's disappeared again."

Polly was still doodling, swinging her legs.

"What?" Polly glanced at them.

"Never mind. Go on with your work, whatever it is. We're going to write you a message." Robin and Kyle huddled in the corner. Polly went back to sketching, whistling "Jingle Bells" under her breath.

Rudy, from the Body Shop, drove his beat-up truck

down the lane hauling a bright blue trailer. An ancient sports car was chained to the trailer. It had Montana plates OWL555. Polly flipped to a clean page and drew the truck, trailer, and all. Two bag men wheeled by, their shopping carts loaded with beer cans, pop bottles, and who knows what hidden in green garbage bags. Maybe they were crooks on the side, and they had people's Christmas presents hidden in there or Isabel's precious stones. But how would they get in the apartment? Polly gave up that idea quickly. The bag men weren't crooks; they were just poor.

Thorn and his girlfriend, the two punks that lived in the furthest house, went by with Safeway bags from the mall.

The Kims pulled up behind the trailer. Thorn, his purple braid hanging down, bent over and talked to Rudy. Polly had nicknamed Thorn's girlfriend "Spiker," because of her orange spiky hairdo. Spiker hurried home with the groceries. Mr. Kim honked the horn of his brown Honda.

Arturo and Rosalie appeared from the back door of the apartment building. Both of them carried heavy garbage bags and struggled towards the trash tins. Suddenly Arturo raised his head, spotted the gathering in the laneway, dropped his bag and ran back into the apartment building. His sister calmly deposited her full bag in the trash and returned for his. Then she disappeared inside.

"Wow!" Polly muttered.

"Hey, she's still alive. She's still with us and hasn't wandered into some other world." Robin came over, leaning her elbows on the railing. "Looks like a community meeting in the back lane."

Mr. Kim honked again.

Rudy rolled up his truck window. Thorn, a shiny ribbon laced through the braid, his earrings glittering in the street light, sauntered towards his house. Spiker watched him come, her freaky orange hair gleaming with gel. Their springer spaniel Brutus had his paws resting on the fence beside her, trying to look like a member of the family. Polly broke the lead on her last pencil trying to catch all the images in the laneway.

"Have you spotted the crooks?" Robin flicked raisins onto Polly's page. Polly grabbed them and shoved them into her mouth. They were cold and hard.

"Who knows? What is Arturo afraid of?" She showed Kyle and Robin the sketch of him running away from the gang in the lane. "Is he allergic to bag men?"

"There's way more poor people in his country, I bet." Robin sighed.

"Maybe he felt sick," Kyle said.

Polly sharpened her pencils, letting the shavings fall onto the frozen brown lawn beneath the willow tree. She scribbled a note on the corner of her sketch – "Arturo runs when he sees the Kims, Rudy, Spiker, and Thorn in the laneway."

"Maybe we should mind our own business." Robin handed Polly the message she and Kyle had written. She shivered and headed for the ladder.

"Let's go to my place. I need cocoa." Polly tucked her sketchbook and the coded message inside her lime-green jacket and followed the others into the warm building. "Besides, I want to think some more about this robbery."

Robin skipped down the rust carpet towards Polly's

apartment. "Maybe you could solve the crime. I can't, 'cause I'm leaving for Hawaii on Thursday night."

"The House of the Elusive Rabbit could help. We could figure stuff out." Polly raced past Robin and unlocked the door with her new keys. "Right now I suspect everyone." She looked from the keys to Kyle's quiet face.

The phone rang. Polly answered it.

"Mr. or Mrs. McDougall, please."

"Who's speaking?" Polly asked. She wasn't supposed to let strangers know she was alone in the apartment.

"Polly, it's Detective Sharon Mills, I wanted to ask your folks if we could come by tonight. We'd like to ask you some more questions. Talk to you and Isabel again about last night."

Polly held the phone to her chest for a moment, gesturing to the others, hopping from one foot to the other. "Sure, Detective Mills. That would be okay. My folks will be home for supper. Do you want them to call you?"

"Why don't we say we'll be there tonight about 7:30?"

"Sure, Detective Mills."

"At your place, then? Have them call here if that's inconvenient, okay?"

"Sure, Detective Mills." Polly hung up the receiver. What a dummy. Sure, Detective Mills. I sounded like a nervous parrot, not a courageous kid. The Courageous Polly McDoodle straightened her back and stamped her foot. She got down the instant cocoa, plugged in the kettle, put three cups and three marshmallows on the counter. Her mind leapt around like a rabbit on hot pavement.

"That's the police. They're coming again tonight. Like I said before, we've got some thinking to do." Polly rubbed her hands together.

"We're collaborators," Kyle whispered. "Investigators."

"We should leave it to the police." Robin frowned and picked at a scab on her knuckle. "It makes me nervous." Robin stirred the marshmallow into her chocolate drink, blew on the top. Some of the foam ran over. "Besides, I have to practice my dance steps for the concert."

"We all need to practice," said Kyle. "Practice is one thing. Solving a crime is another."

Polly cleared a place on the kitchen table. She grabbed some paper and a ruler from her dad's desk in the corner of the living room. "Don't wimp out, Robin. You want to help Isabel get her stuff back, don't you?" She reached up to her neck and pulled out the heliotrope on its chain.

Kyle moved to the kitchen window and stared down the lane, sipping his hot chocolate, tracing the words "Elusive Rabbit" in the frost on the inside.

"Are you going to clam up again, Kyle?" Polly looked up from her map, notes and sketches.

"I've got to go." Robin put her mug in the sink and wiped her chocolate moustache off with a paper towel. "Maybe I could help until my plane leaves, though. As long as it's not dangerous."

"Count me in. It's like a puzzle." Kyle came to the table, his eyes serious behind the thick glasses. "This is no kid's game we're playing, though. Let's not forget that."

5. Another Day, Another Robbery

"WHERE DID YOU GET THE APARTMENT KEYS, KYLE?"
Polly asked after Robin had left. He stared at her. "I
need to know. It's important." Kyle pursed his lips like a
fish and exhaled.

"Otherwise, you are a suspect." Polly chewed the top
of her pencil.

"Oh!"

"How did you get those keys?" Her heart was thumping. Please, don't be anything mysterious, she whispered
inside her head. Please just be my old buddy, Kyle the
Clam.

"Okay! Okay! My dad's the head of the Tenants'
Association. He has a master key and keys to all the suites.
I'm not supposed to tell." Kyle hung his head. "I borrowed
them to make copies at the mall because I didn't want you
getting into trouble losing your keys like that."

Polly heaved a sigh of relief. At least that was one
puzzle solved. Maybe having bad things happening
made you suspicious of everyone. A sudden vision of
Arturo flashed into her mind. Maybe he wasn't cold and
distant at all. Maybe he was suspicious, even of kids.

Maybe he didn't trust anyone. Poor Arturo. Polly had trusted nearly everyone up until the robbery, up until yesterday. She would have to lighten up, be the Mostly Trusting McDoodle, again.

Kyle sat working at the table while Polly put frozen fish and chips in the oven and chopped cabbage for coleslaw. Her dad would make his incredible McDougall dressing when he came home.

Polly joined Kyle at the table, looking over his shoulder. He'd taken her drawings with all their buildings, people, cars and rabbits running or sitting around the outside and spread them out. With a ruler and pencil he'd drawn a map of the same space, complete with names, street numbers. He looked up and grinned. "Logic and intuition. We'll need both."

Polly scratched her head. "You're a grownup disguised as a kid, Kyle. Did you know that?"

Kyle gazed at her with a quizzical expression on his face, head cocked on a slant, straw hair sticking out like porcupine quills. His dumb red shirt had come untucked. Someone should tell the kid that sixth grade boys don't wear red flannel shirts.

"We need a list of clues and suspects," he said.

"It can't be anyone in this apartment building. We've lived here for ages." Polly doodled on the corner of the nearest drawing. Another elusive rabbit emerged.

"It feels that way," Kyle said. "But Isabel and the DeCostas are new. Some of the nurses on the third floor moved in in September."

There was a loud bang at the door and it was flung open.

"We've been robbed." Robin's round face was flushed

and splotchy. "They took Mom's jewelry and the plane tickets from Dad's dresser drawer. And my recorder."

Polly's mouth opened in surprise. She dropped her pencil and stared at Robin. Her best friend's eyes looked scared, darker somehow. Polly felt suddenly like she'd taken too fast an elevator ride. This was too much. She dashed over and grabbed Robin by the shoulders. "When did they get in − while we were at school? Do we have to skip school and keep watch?"

"All small stuff," Kyle said. "They only take portable stuff. That's very interesting."

"Interesting? It's terrible! We have to buy new tickets. That's expensive − and my mom's crying."

"Must have broken in during the day." Polly frowned. "We've got to stop them somehow. Most of the people in the apartment building work or go to school." She stared at the maps they had drawn, thinking about who the crooks could be. "Who could break in during the day?"

Robin pulled up a kitchen chair. "The police are on their way. Dad's stomping around like an old bear. I want my recorder back." She sifted through all the drawings and Kyle's map and looked at Polly. "This is getting serious."

"I wonder if they used my keys to get into the apartment building. But that wouldn't get them into your place."

"Any signs of forced entry? What about the patio door?" Kyle sat beside Robin, his black notebook open and his pencil poised.

"Some friends you are. All you can talk about is how it was done, who did it. I've been robbed, you turkeys!

Wait until something of yours is stolen," Robin shouted. "This is no Encyclopedia Brown mystery here. They've got my recorder!"

"Okay!" Polly leaned towards Robin. "We're trying to help, okay."

Robin jumped up and circled the room, then threw herself on the old maroon couch. The springs howled. The three friends flashed funny looks at each other, and broke out laughing.

"Dumb old couch," Polly sputtered.

"Dumb old crooks," Robin screeched.

Kyle bent double holding his stomach as if in pain. His laugh gurgled in his throat.

"He even laughs like a clam." Robin pointed at Kyle. The three of them collapsed in a heap of legs, arms, and wiggly bodies on the floor.

"What's all the racket?" Shawn dropped his massive hockey bag in the hall. "It's a wonder the Beamishes don't complain."

"About you dropping heavy objects on their heads," Polly pointed at his hockey bag. The quiet couple downstairs with their cats and computers had never complained once about any noise from the apartment above them. "Take pity on them, brother."

"What about all the noise from you and your little friends." He sauntered down the hall towards his room. "You better tidy up – Mom and Dad will be home any minute for supper."

Polly picked herself up off the floor, scooped all the loose drawings, maps, and codes into an empty file folder from Dad's desk and handed it to Kyle, as he and Robin left. "Here, keep this!"

She rubbed the heliotrope between her thumb and finger and disappeared into her room. As she pulled the drapes closed she spotted Thorn walking quickly across the parking lot back to the lane. He slowed as he passed the tree fort, looking warily around before moving on. What was he doing hanging around their place? Polly stretched out on the bed to think about the robberies. The last thing she heard was Kyle upstairs practicing his concert piece.

"HONEY, ARE YOU IN THERE?" Dad's voice was muffled by the door. "Supper's on the table."

Polly sat up and rubbed her eyes. "Coming."

"Are you all right, honey?" Dad asked.

"Uh-huh." Polly tidied the bedspread, ran a comb through her messy hair, and opened the door.

Her mother looked up from the end of the table. "You've got creases in your cheek from sleeping so hard. Are you sure you're okay?"

"She was fine when I got home," Shawn said in between giant mouthfuls of coleslaw. "She and her buddies were rolling on the floor in fits of glee."

"It wasn't a fit of glee," Polly cried. "Weinsteins were robbed this afternoon. We were cheering up Robin."

"Beamishes had their laptop, CD player, and tape deck taken." Dad speared another hunk of fish. "Nobody's safe."

"Do we need a tenants' meeting?" Polly's mom paced the kitchen floor. "We could discuss changing the locks. Let's put up notices in the hallways and the laundry room."

Dad wiped his mouth with his napkin. "Good idea, right after the game. It's just starting."

Shawn gulped the last of his milk and shoved his plate away. "Could Polly do my dishes? I need to watch the game – pick up pointers from the pros."

Polly was drawing her french fries through a puddle of ketchup on the edge of her plate. Her napkin had doodles of rabbits and giant locks all over it. Her pencil was tucked under her plate.

"I got supper. The police detective phoned you," she said to her parents. "They are coming at 7:30 to talk to me and Isabel again. Kyle and I are going out to look for clues right now."

Her mother was standing across the table from her. "Polly, don't go poking into things. Curiosity killed the cat, you know." She rescued the plate, saw the pencil marks on the table where Polly's doodles had gone over the edge.

"I wish you'd find something less messy to do with all your energy. Too bad you quit dancing lessons."

"I'm no good at dancing...I like to draw." Why couldn't her mom leave her be? Polly didn't want to be organized.

The pre-game show blared from the living room. Shawn and Dad were already ensconced on the couch.

"Maybe you and I could go to mother-daughter aerobics this winter. I want you to keep fit. We don't want you turning into a couch potato." Mom picked up her latest crochet project and curled up on the big tan chair. Her hands flew. "Dishes, Shawn."

"I'll do them. I'll do them," Shawn grumbled. "At the end of the period, I promise."

Polly watched her mother's competent fingers. She felt awkward around a mother who was a dancer and a fitness teacher and a needleworker, and a brother who was a hockey star. Polly reached through her open collar and rubbed the heliotrope. The Frightfully Fit McDoodle flew away.

6. Too Many Suspects

POLLY SPOTTED THE ELUSIVE RABBIT AGAIN AS SHE came back from walking George. The poor rabbit was still wearing a white fur coat on a snowless evening in December, needing desperately to be invisible to hunters or hawks, and if not invisible at least elusive, able to run across parking lots when people were sleeping, to nibble in the park when the kids were in school.

"Oh, rabbit," Polly whispered as she crept closer, "I understand how you feel." She could see it shaking, its whiskers quivering. A twig snapped under Polly's heel, George growled, and the rabbit streaked past the willow tree, past the garbage tins, the parked cars, down the lane toward the park.

"Hey, TC2," Polly called after the disappearing rabbit. Then she continued talking out loud more to herself than anything, "I worked out the coded message Robin and Kyle gave me. *T-W2-R2-H2-U-L2-T C2-W-I-I-U-U2.* That's your code name."

A puzzled magpie squawked at her. She pressed her lips together and took George home.

"Are you coming to work on your parents' picture?" Isabel asked.

Polly mumbled something about going outside with the kids. Polly didn't look Isabel in the eye.

"See you at 7:30?" Isabel's voice hesitated. "With the two detectives."

Polly's lime-green ski jacket made crinkly noises as she ran back down the hallway towards the exit. She glanced at the coat's neon brightness, listened to its crackling. Then she slipped into the apartment and rummaged in the front hall closet for something less loud. She needed to be elusive, like the rabbit, if she was going hunting for clues.

The hockey fans were glued to the TV, munching popcorn and making encouraging noises.

"Move it, you guys. Get the lead out of your skates," Mom shouted.

"Pass the puck, pass it," Shawn yelled. Polly shoved the coats and jackets back and forth looking for the right thing to wear. Finally she discovered a tattered flannel-lined brown and green camouflage jacket of Shawn's hanging in the back of the closet, an old pair of black gloves of her mom's, and a navy blue toque abandoned in the bottom of the box of winter stuff.

"They're organizing a ringette league at the community centre," Mom said while the commercial droned on. "Think I'll sign Polly up."

"Oh, Mom, she'll fall and sprain her ankle like she did in soccer last year," Shawn said. "Leave her be."

Polly stood hidden in the hallway in Shawn's ragged jacket and toque. The smell of pine needles from the Christmas tree filled the air with a country perfume.

This was the first Christmas she could remember when the important thing wasn't getting presents. She was too old for that. She wanted something else from Christmas this year. Something that presents wouldn't give her. She wasn't sure what it was. But digging into this robbery, trying to help Isabel, working with Kyle was part of it. She felt like an older Polly was standing just outside the door, watching to see how she'd make out. Maybe there really was an Invisible Polly McDoodle after all.

"Ted, I'm worried about Polly. I don't want her sitting in the house all winter, doodling, watching TV. She needs exercise or she'll grow too self-centred and neurotic. All she does is draw, draw, draw. She has no idea how hard it is to be an artist. She'll get hurt for sure when she doesn't make it. I know how that feels."

"Polly's okay, Jan," Dad said. "Kids are more resilient nowadays – they bounce back. If being an artist doesn't work out, well...."

"Ted, you don't know what you're talking about. Kids get their hopes up, build castles in the air. I don't want to see her dreams shattered. I don't want...."

"Look at him go," Shawn hollered. "The goalie's out to lunch. Wow, what a goal!"

Polly tiptoed to the apartment door, carefully snicked it shut and made her way down the hall. She didn't understand what her mom was going on about, she didn't understand at all. She shook her head to clear it and bounded down the stairs.

Kyle waited by the back door. "What kept you?" He pushed outside, bundled in his navy pea jacket and old red-checked hunter's hat.

"Jeez, Kyle, that hat looks dumb."

"I wouldn't talk," Kyle snorted.

Polly studied her own outfit and giggled. "Where's Robin?"

"Out."

"We'll have to go without her."

Kyle climbed the ladder to the tree fort where he grabbed his flashlight. Polly followed him. She shoved her sketchbook and a pencil into the huge pocket of her brother's cast-off coat.

"How many people know your dad has a set of master keys?"

Kyle shrugged his shoulders. Running footsteps echoed down the lane. Polly dropped to the pavement. Kyle followed and turned the full glare of his flashlight in the direction of the sound. A full chorus of dogs barked. A car door slammed and tires tore up some gravel.

Kyle and Polly sprinted down the lane close to the fence. Whoever had been there had disappeared. The two friends leaned against the Kims's cedar fence, panting. The pencil jabbed Polly's side so she moved it to the top pocket of the jacket. She touched Kyle's arm, put a finger to her lips, then chuckled. Hushing Kyle was like telling a rock to sit still.

Rudy, the Body Shop owner, stood in the doorway of his garage, smoking a foul-smelling cigar, a dirty white sweatshirt stretched over his beer belly. Machinery roared inside the garage. The noise stopped suddenly. Rudy threw the cigar down, ground it out with the heel of his boot, and went back inside, quickly closing the door behind him. Polly shuddered. That man gave her the creeps.

A back porch light went on, flooding the Kims's backyard. Mr. Kim and his son Jimmy came out carrying something that seemed to be heavy between them. As Kyle and Polly watched they dug a huge hole in the corner of their garden.

Shovelful after shovelful of dirt thudded onto a pile. Polly peered through the fence. The Kims's black cat jumped on Kyle's shoulder, its claws digging into his flesh.

"Humpf!" Kyle howled in pain. The Kims dropped their shovels and started toward the back fence where Polly and Kyle stood. The two of them lit out down the lane toward the park. As they waited at the end of the block behind a giant elm on Thorn and Spiker's boulevard for a couple of cars to pass, a siren wailed on Kingsway. Polly caught her breath and stared in the punks' kitchen window. Spiker, orange hair and dangling earrings, purple eye shadow and garish red lipstick, stood doing dishes in time to the loud banging of heavy metal music. Polly poked Kyle in the ribs and pointed at the domestic scene. "Even punks eat and do laundry, I guess. I wonder what she'd look like without all that goop."

"You could draw her."

Thorn's ugly brown van turned the corner. Polly pulled Kyle across to the pocket park. "Quick, I want to watch this!"

Kyle climbed onto the park bench in the shade of the pine tree. Polly leaped up too and stood beside him. Through the branches they could see everything in the laneway without being seen. They had been pretty sneaky so far, pretty elusive. The Incredibly Elusive

McDoodle and Clay, Private Investigators. Polly could see the brass sign in front of their office.

Thorn got out of his van, walked around to the back and opened the doors. He carried a plastic grocery bag filled with stuff into his own house. He and Spiker stood talking for several minutes. Polly was just about to give up when Thorn came back out, shouted something into the van, grabbed a box of stuff and took it over to Rudy's garage, knocked on the door and was admitted.

The red MG with the giant blond-haired man came whipping around the corner, nearly running into Thorn's van which wasn't quite pulled off the lane. A huge plant wrapped in florists' green bags sat perched on the passenger seat.

"Escape of the killer tomato!" Kyle poked Polly.

While all this was going on, a small figure dropped out of the back of the van, ran across Ninth Street and disappeared down a laneway. Whoever it was had been carrying a dark gym bag or sack which banged against his right side as he ran.

Thorn's dog started moaning. Spiker opened the window and hollered. "Shut up, Brutus, for crying out loud. He'll be home in a minute."

Kyle pushed his sleeve up and showed Polly the time.

Polly mentally added several things to her list of clues and questions. "What did the Kims bury? What's going on at Rudy's? Who was the runner? What has Thorn got to do with Rudy?" She promised herself as she hopped down from the bench that she would add more detail to her bird's eye view of the neighbourhood later after every one had gone home. She might draw a picture of Spiker like Kyle had suggested.

Thorn came out of Rudy's place and nearly ran into Kyle and Polly.

"What are you two kids doing here?"

Polly kept walking as if he hadn't spoken to her. Her heart pounded, flipped and banged in her chest.

"Mind your own business!" Thorn barked.

"Leave us alone!" Kyle shouted.

"This laneway isn't yours," Polly blurted.

"Stay at your own end of the block or else." Thorn moved toward them, his head thrust forward like a mean wrestler on Saturday TV.

Polly turned on her heel and ran as fast as she could. She could hear Kyle's runners crunching the gravel behind her. She didn't stop until she came to the base of the willow tree. She clutched at the tree for a minute to catch her breath.

She reached under the bulky jacket and touched the heliotrope. It felt warm, snuggled close to her chest, next to her skin. Kyle caught up to her, a frown puckering his forehead, his hands shoved deep in his pockets. He kept glancing back down the lane, kicking pebbles onto the laneway.

"Boy, what's his problem?" Polly whispered as they approached the back door where two police officers sat in a car.

Kyle nodded in their direction. "That's why Thorn didn't come after us...he could see the cruiser. Make sure you tell them about Thorn bugging us."

"You tell them." Polly punched him on the arm. "McDoodle and Clay, private eyes. You'll have to talk, though."

Kyle nodded his head in agreement and sprinted up the stairs in front of her. The two uniformed officers followed.

She, Kyle, and the police officers crowded into the vestibule, taking off their coats and hanging them up.

Her dad was making coffee and tea, the two detectives were standing in the middle of the living room, and her mom was directing traffic, when Polly opened the door.

"That chair is quite comfortable, Detective Mills, Detective Anderson. Make yourselves at home. Shawn, roll the TV down the corridor...watch out for the wallpaper." She tidied magazines and pulled dining room chairs into a circle. "Oh, good, here's Polly and Kyle. Where have you two been? Your faces are all red like you've been running. Playing?"

Isabel came through the open door. Polly's mom settled Isabel in the corner of the couch. Then she took orders for coffee, tea and juice and delivered them to Polly's dad in the kitchen.

The two uniformed officers sat down, one on the folding chair and the skinny young one on the kitchen stool. He balanced a pad on his knee.

"We were wondering about having the police come and talk to the Tenants' Association next month about security." Polly's mom stood in the kitchen doorway holding a tray of fruit and cheese. "This whole thing has caught us off guard."

"Might be a good idea," Detective Anderson said. Polly went and sat beside Isabel. The room felt too crowded to Polly. She pulled out the colourful heliotrope, letting it glisten in the light from the table lamp. She swallowed and turned to Isabel.

"I wish you would take this back."

"Now Polly, I told you before I don't want it back. It would look silly on a big woman like me."

"But...but," Polly stuttered.

"I thought Kyle was the clam, not you." Isabel put a freckled hand on Polly's arm. "I don't blame you, child, for the robbery. I never double-lock the door. I lived in a little town all my life. Stop your stewing." Then she whispered, "Come over later to work on your folks' painting, okay? Besides you look like you have a few things to talk over. What's been happening?"

Polly moved closer to Isabel and heaved a big sigh of relief. She felt safe beside Isabel. Safe and something else...welcomed, maybe. It made her more determined than ever to help get Isabel's gems back. She and Kyle would solve this mystery, help the police any way they could.

"I think you should know that another apartment building, two blocks from here, on the other side of Ninth Street, has suffered a rash of robberies as well this week." Detective Anderson cleared his throat, popped a cough drop in his mouth, fidgeted with his pen collection in his pocket and continued talking. "As I said last night, we suspect a small gang. It's high priority that we figure out their modus operandi."

"Every criminal has a way of working, that's the 'modus operandi,'" Kyle told Polly in a stage whisper.

"I know that." Then Polly asked a question. "Have you figured out how the criminals are getting in to the apartments yet?"

"In some cases we think the doors were not secured."

Here Detective Anderson stared hard at Polly. "In other cases we have found footprints on the balconies, or traces of prying tools by the doorjamb."

"Crooks use credit cards," Shawn said. "You just slide the plastic...."

"That's enough. We've some questions," Detective Mills interrupted Shawn in mid-sentence. She nodded to the young uniformed officer with the notebook. "Polly, would you go over the details of your movements last night one more time." Detective Mills stroked her chin. Her blonde hair was cropped close to her head like a cap. Her blue eyes blinked as she asked questions. "We are trying to fix the time of the robbery."

In a firm, clear voice Polly told the detectives everything she could remember. George sat at her feet, his tongue lolling out of his mouth, groaning occasionally, as if agreeing with her. She scratched his furry head.

Kyle sat in the corner listening intently as if he was trying to memorize the order of events. Isabel nudged Polly when she stammered over the door locking scene.

"Officer, as we told you before, we've never been fussy about locks," Isabel said when she spotted the detectives' raised eyebrows. "I guess all that will change now. Our days of trusting everyone are gone."

"We'll bring good days back," Kyle muttered.

Polly grinned. Maybe Kyle didn't talk much, but when it came to something important he knew what to say. But could they really do that? Would they ever really trust anyone again?

7. Notes In Class

POLLY, CAN'T HELP. PARENTS SAY DANGER. SORRY, *Your friend forever, Robin*, the pink note said.

Polly sat in Jonesy's social studies class Wednesday morning trying to concentrate, staring at the note in her folder. At the bottom of the page was scrawled their code for the rabbit, TC2.

Kyle glanced up at Polly and winked. He was busy solving the complicated questions in the back of the math book. He said it helped him think. That or practicing the piano probably let his brain loose to work on the robberies. Just like doodling freed Polly's brain.

Outside the window a cold wind blew, making the Christmas lights on the giant blue spruce rattle and snap. The caretaker, wrapped in a gigantic coat, wobbled on a ladder, replacing burnt-out bulbs. His mittened hands fumbled with the string of blue lights. Something about his hands struggling with the lights made Polly feel helpless, made her feel small, made her want to go and help him. The Wistful Polly McDoodle sighed.

"Polly, what about family life in Greece?" Jonesy

stood beside her. While she had been looking out the window she'd been doodling – a white rabbit climbing a ladder. Polly bit her lip and searched her mind for some fact about Greece. The classroom stayed quieter than a library as the kids and Jonesy waited.

"I hope you aren't still wrapped up in all the burglaries at your end of the block," Jonesy chided. "It's not like any of you are involved.... Not many crooks in this class," he chuckled.

Polly had informed the whole class of the goings-on in her apartment building during news time earlier. Robin had added lots of details. She loved reporting things. Even if she didn't like getting dirty, she sure liked telling all she knew.

"If Greek families didn't want girl babies they put them in a pot and left them in a field to die," Polly blurted.

"Boy, are you in a gruesome mood or what," Robin whispered over her shoulder.

"Maybe Kyle could elucidate on some of the more positive aspects of family life in the early Greek home." Jonesy seemed to be picking on the kids from the apartment building. Polly shook her head. It's like he knows our brains are focused somewhere else.

Kyle blushed and put his notebook over the sheet of math problems. "They had bread and weak wine for breakfast. The boys went to school but the girls had to stay home and do chores. Slaves did all the heavy work."

"Would you like to add anything, Arturo?" Jonesy asked slowly and clearly. He leaned his tall angular frame against the board, getting chalk dust on his ratty tweed jacket. His Adam's apple bounced.

Arturo had been sitting in his desk near the front of the class, listening closely to what everyone said, his head tilted to one side. Now his head was drooping over an open book.

"Greece is where democracia started. Democracia is a precious thing, my papa said." His face flushed. "But even in democracia there are bad people...." Arturo's skin looked dull yellow. "Please, sir, I do not feel good." Polly was afraid he might puke right there. Something had upset him terribly. "I go home, yes?" Arturo stood up beside his desk, his left hand grasping the back of the seat as if it was the only solid thing in the room.

"I could take him to the nurse," Kyle said.

"I could take him home," Polly volunteered. She flashed an encouraging smile at the boy, hoping he would understand how much she and Kyle wanted to help.

Arturo glanced back and forth from Jonesy to Polly and Kyle. He lifted his free hand toward his mouth. "I may be excused?" It was a question, but Arturo ran down the aisle and out the door without waiting for an answer.

Jonesy shook his head. "Poor kid," he said. "Go after him, Kyle. See he's okay."

The kids in the class turned to each other and chattered. Jonesy ambled to his desk and straightened his papers, checked in his messy planner. Polly thought, watching him, Jonesy forgets what he's doing if someone interrupts him.

"We were talking about Greece, Mr. Jones," Robin said. "Arturo said that's where democracy started."

"Oh, yes." Jonesy walked back to the board, picked

up a piece of chalk. "That was a good point. We in Canada can thank the Greeks and the Romans for our form of government." With one last glance at the open door, the silent corridor, he turned back to the lesson.

Kyle tiptoed in and sat in his seat.

Polly, turned sideways in her chair, whispered, "Where's Arturo?"

Kyle shrugged. "Gone."

The recess bell went. Jonesy hurried from the room.

"What do you mean, gone?" Polly asked Kyle as the two friends walked to the door.

"He's gone, that's all," Kyle said again. "He's not in the bathroom, not in the hall, not in the sick room. The secretary didn't see him."

"He must be really sick," Polly said.

"I thought he looked kind of green," Robin added.

"Could be something he ate," Kyle said.

Polly shook her head from side to side. "I don't think so. I think it's something else. We were talking about Greece,... Mr. Jones was teasing us about being crooks.... What could upset him like that? Why did he drop his bag of garbage when he saw all the people in the alley? Why did he pull Rosalie away from us when we were talking about the robbery?"

"Maybe he's got malaria or some terrible disease," Robin said. "I used to bring up every time I ate choco-late. Maybe he's allergic to chocolate."

"Maybe he's scared," Kyle whispered and waved at a couple of his buddies. He ran to catch up to them, leav-ing Polly chewing her lip, trying to figure out what or who Arturo was afraid of.

Polly and Robin went through the double doors to

the playground, and spotted Arturo running across the park to the laneway behind their apartment building.

Rosalie, tumbling out with a flock of third graders, ran a few steps, spotted her brother, and trotted after him.

"Wait, Rosalie!" Polly shouted. "Come on, Robin, we've got to talk to her."

"If it's about the robberies...." Robin hesitated.

"Your brother's sick." Polly huffed as she caught up to Rosalie.

Rosalie tried to run away but Robin grabbed her arm. "It's okay, Rosalie."

"Maybe we can help?" Polly reached a hand out to her. "Is he in some kind of trouble?"

"He says not to talk to you. He says you think you hot shots. Don't trust anyone. He says we have to take care of ourselves." Rosalie pulled away and ran, tears blinding her.

"What's going on?" Kyle joined Robin and Polly by the empty soccer net.

"It's Arturo," Polly said. "He may be in deep trouble. He's told Rosalie not to talk to us. There's more to this than we think. It may be part of the mystery."

"My dad says we should stay out of it. It's the police's job." Robin walked away.

"Fine for you – you're going on vacation," Polly blurted, following her. "My folks want to help the police, and so do I."

Robin pushed the toe of her shoe in the dirt making a hole. "I shouldn't have told my parents about us working on the robbery, but I got so excited. I want to help get my recorder back but I can't." Then she pouted. "You know what my folks are like...." Her voice trailed off.

Polly studied Robin's forlorn face and knew her old buddy Robin was scared, glad her folks had stopped her. She was still Polly's best friend, but she wasn't going to be much help.

"Hey, we'll fill you in on everything when you get back from Hawaii." Kyle slapped his ugly old mitts together and let off a cloud of dust. The three giggled and walked to the water fountain. "Elusive Rabbit, TC2," they whispered.

Polly spied Thorn and Spiker's brown van slowly cruising by the school yard.

"That's one really bad dude," Kyle said under his breath.

"Just because he dresses weird?" Polly asked. "Just because he hollered at us?"

"You don't have the whole story," Kyle said sharply.

"So tell us, Clam." Robin poked him.

Kyle pulled a handful of sunflower seeds from his pocket and shoved them in his mouth. He shook his head and walked over to a gang of boys playing penny toss by the school wall.

"You've got more secrets than the FBI," Robin yelled after him.

"He makes me mad." Polly kicked an empty juice container in the direction of the trash barrel, bent to toss it in, and blood rushed to her head, making her feel dizzy. Having Rosalie, that little kid with her big sad eyes, staring at her, saying things about Polly and Kyle and Robin not being trustworthy, made Polly feel funny. Maybe Rosalie had a iceberg inside her. Just like Isabel.

On her way back to class she stopped by Mrs. Stock's

room. "I think Rosalie went home to see if her brother was all right. He looked sick."

"Oh, Polly, I'm so glad to see you." Mrs. Stock pulled her into the class. "I've been worried about Rosalie the last couple of days. Do you know what's going on?"

Polly shook her head. She couldn't very well say she and Kyle and Robin knew nothing about Arturo and Rosalie. If they had problems, the House of the Elusive Rabbit would be the last to know. It looked as if Rosalie and Arturo wouldn't tell them anything anyway. That hurt.

"Could you take a note home to her mother?"

Polly nodded. She stared at the top of Rosalie's desk. Rosalie, like all the other third grade kids, had a bright folder with worksheets in it. A nicely crayoned picture was glued to the front of the red cover. The drawing was of a huge white rabbit with a plaid waistcoat and a polkadot bow tie. The rabbit's trousers were red like the cover and his feet and ears were brown, just like the elusive rabbit in the park. Rosalie must have seen the rabbit or else she wouldn't know his ears and feet were still brown.

"Polly," Mrs. Stock handed her a note in a blue envelope. "Do you think Mrs. DeCosta understands enough English?"

Shaking her head to clear it, Polly blinked. "She's going to night classes at the high school."

She tiptoed into her classroom and down the aisle past Kyle's place and dropped a note on his desk. "TC2, meet me at the tree," she whispered as she sat down, Mrs. Stock's note to Mrs. DeCosta burning a hole in her jeans pocket.

Jonesy, marking papers, raised his eyebrows and gazed at Polly. She told him and the rest of the class about Arturo and Rosalie taking off at recess.

"I wish you kids would explain the rules to our Salvadoran students. How would you feel if you were in a strange school, in a strange country using a strange language?" Jonesy sighed and put the papers away.

Polly reached for the heliotrope hanging at her throat. The skin on her forehead felt tight like a drum as she thought of Rosalie's dark eyes and Arturo's drooping head. She had to do something to change their view of the kids in the apartment building. It wouldn't solve the crime but it would make her feel better.

"Ready, class...the dress rehearsal for the concert starts in a few minutes. Clean off your desks, make sure all papers and belongings are put away. Polly, bring the paints."

Polly walked to the back of the room and picked up the cardboard box filled with tempera paints. One of her rabbits and two of her trees decorated the corner of the box. Nobody else doodled rabbits and trees like she did, so where did Rosalie get a full page drawing of the elusive rabbit? Polly didn't remember leaving any lying about. Lots of little ones like these on the box, but not many done on big sheets of art paper.

"Wake up, Polly, I want to lock the door," Jonesy called. "The principal says there have been robberies in the whole neighbourhood, not just your apartment building. The school could be next." Polly hugged the box to her chest and hurried past him.

In the hallway by the principal's office stood a rack of

pink, blue, and yellow information sheets about all the junior highs. She picked up two – one about Kirby on the south side with its arts programs, and the other about plain old Central Junior High down the block. Maybe if her folks read them they'd understand why she wanted to go to Kirby. Life seemed too complex right now for a kid. She had to pick a school, solve a crime, help Arturo, and finish a painting – all before Christmas. She had to become the Tough-Job Juggler McDoodle.

Polly trotted down the lane after practice, humming "Frosty the Snowman," hoping for snow. Snow covers everything, hiding the ugly junk, changing the dreary browns and greys of a city into pure white. She loved sitting inside, warm and cosy, staring at the trees with clouds of snow on their branches, cars topped with a thick icing of white. It was beautiful, a winter wonderland. She loved rolling in snow, throwing it, making snow sculptures. How she longed for snow. It didn't feel much like Christmas without snow. Polly McDoodle, TV Weather Woman, predicts snow, snow, snow.

Chief, the German shepherd tied by Rudy's garage, barked sharply. Brutus, the springer, woofed from Thorn's backyard. Mr. Kim stood on his back porch in his shirt-sleeves defying the cold wind, surveying the square space, now neatly flat and raked, where last night he and his son had buried something. What were they up to? Lights shone from behind roller blinds covering the Twins' greenhouse; a smell of humus, wet plants, and fertilizer lingered in the lane close to it. She really didn't suspect the Twins of anything. They'd never set foot in the apartment that she could remember. The

Kims were friends with the Razis, though. So they'd been in the apartment building. Rudy, no. Spiker, no.

Thorn had had a bachelor suite on the ground floor back when she was a little kid, Shawn had reminded her.

Polly stared at the balconies and windows of the apartment building. Except for the Beamishes' Siamese perched on the iron railing, all was quiet. The student nurses, the university students, the Weinsteins, the Clays, Isabel, the McDougalls, the caretaker, the Razis, and the DeCostas; no potential robbers in there. It couldn't be an inside job, no matter what Detective Anderson said. She kept coming back to Thorn. And something didn't fit about Arturo, some picture she had of him just didn't fit.

Polly took Mrs. Stock's note from her pocket and slid it into the DeCostas' mail box. The Not So Brave Polly McDoodle shivered. She should deliver the note but she couldn't. She didn't know why – she just couldn't. But she knew one thing for sure: she had to do something about Arturo and Rosalie. She hated having people not trust her. It was worse than being invisible, much worse.

8. McDoodle and Clay, Detectives

THE PHONE RANG AS SHE OPENED THE DOOR. SHE raced to pick it up.

"Hello! Hello?" No one spoke. There was a click and the dial tone returned.

That's funny, the same thing happened last night when Shawn got it.

A muffled bang sounded at the door. Polly jumped.

"Who is it?"

"Kyle." He was bundled in his usual disreputable-looking outfit.

"The phone just rang and no one was there."

Kyle nodded his head so rapidly his toque fell off. "It's happened at our place, too." He waved her towards the door.

"Why don't we stay in? I wanted to report on our investigation. I've got a couple of more clues," Polly said.

Kyle reached for her brother's old jacket and tossed it at her. "Me, too."

Polly shrugged, picked up Kyle's toque, threw it at his head, and pulled on the jacket he'd tossed at her. All this was accomplished in silence.

"Boy, if being elusive meant making no noise, you'd be the winner," Polly teased. "I gather we're going out. McDoodle and Clay on stakeout?"

"Sorry." Kyle led the way to the fort. He reached his hand into one of the old squirrel holes in the thick base of the tree and lifted out a piece of art paper, torn from a coil binder.

Polly stared at it.

"What is it, a new code? You brought me out in this cold to look at a new code." On the list were numbers, initials, and more numbers. "I don't get it." She scratched her chin. "Unless it's the paper. It looks like a piece from Isabel's sketch book."

They were standing shoulder to shoulder in the bright, floodlit parking lot. Miniature lights on the fir tree blipped on and off. Kyle scrambled up the rope ladder and turned to help Polly. He flashed the beam from his huge lantern on the paper which he had spread on the upturned crate. "Look at this carefully," he grinned.

"Okay. So it says *IA 204 425 0138, BB 101 425 2040*. Wait a minute. I get it. It's the initials of people in the apartment block, their apartment numbers and these must be their telephone numbers."

The two of them stared at each other.

"There's a red tick beside Isabel's, and one beside *BB* and *W* – for Weinstein, I bet. Those are the apartments that have been robbed."

"The crooks phone ahead to find out if the place is empty." Kyle spoke with excitement. "Then they break in."

"This is evidence. Do you think there are fingerprints?" Polly jumped up and down. "That's not all. Listen to my news. Rosalie had one of my rabbits as a notebook cover. The rabbit had brown ears, just like the elusive one down the block. What I can't figure out is where she got it? Who gave it to her?"

"Was it on art paper like this?" Kyle asked. "I keep feeling those kids are involved somehow. I don't want to believe that, but I do."

The McDougalls' car pulled into its parking spot. Polly's folks emerged carrying big shopping bags, giggling. Polly's mom directed traffic. "Ted, take the small presents and put them in our closet. We'll hide these others in the..." she whispered.

Kyle tugged at his ear.

"I've got to go in," Polly said. "It's my turn to set the table."

"Okay." Kyle pulled a handful of sunflower seeds out of his pocket. "Tomorrow after school we've got some investigating to do."

"I've been thinking about Arturo and Rosalie. Rosalie said Arturo didn't want her talking to us. Said we couldn't be trusted. Someone is filling his head with bad ideas about us. Either that or we ignored them too long. I could kick myself, I've been so unconscious. I've been the Unconscious Polly McDoodle. If they're in trouble...."

"We've got to help. If they're in trouble you're thinking it could be our fault." Kyle popped the seeds in his mouth. He lifted the lid of his crate to put his flashlight away. "No!" Kyle shouted.

His voice sounded like he had been punched hard in the stomach. Polly dropped to the floor beside him and looked in his trunk. None of his stuff was there. Every one of his D. and D. books, figures and dice, the comic books and cards were gone.

A note written in block letters filled the bottom of the box.

MIND YOUR OWN BUSINESS OR YOU'LL GET HURT.

They knelt back on their heels, shoved their hands deep in their pockets to keep warm. Polly shivered.

"Oh Jeez, oh heck, oh bummer," Kyle moaned.

"This makes me angry," Polly said. "I don't like this at all. The 'mind your own business' stuff – that makes me really mad. Where have I heard that before?"

"The note is intimidating."

"What?" Polly looked puzzled.

"Trying to shut people up or putting on pressure to make people do stuff they think is wrong – that's intimidation," Kyle explained. "Thorn tried to intimidate me," he added.

"When?"

"A couple of weeks ago. He cornered me in the Wizard's Castle." Kyle gulped. "Said he'd tell my folks I hung out playing video games in the arcade. Said he'd leave a note on the dashboard."

"Wow!"

"Wanted me to give him keys to the place." Kyle's face was beet red. "Said he'd left stuff in the basement a few years ago, wanted it back."

"Did you let him have the keys?" Polly's mind raced ahead.

"No."

"Did he tell your folks?"

"No, I did." Kyle dropped his head onto his chest. "I got a half-hour lecture, and had my allowance cut."

"Kyle, don't you see how important this is?" Polly banged her left fist into her right palm. "You stupid clam, why didn't you tell me?"

"Polly! Polly! Are you in the fort?" Her mother called from the balcony.

Polly leaped for the ladder and scurried down.

"Polly!" her mother said as they sat down to barbe-cued Safeway chicken at the table. "I talked to the Weinsteins at the mall."

Polly chewed her lip. Oh, oh, here it comes.

Her dad looked concerned, but he kept on shovelling corn and potatoes into his mouth.

"Weinsteins said they had forbidden Robin to get involved in some detective work you and Kyle are doing...something to do with the robberies."

Polly cleared her throat and looked to her brother for help.

Shawn, chomping on a chicken leg, was not looking at her. Her dad put his fork down.

"The police are dealing with the case quite well, Polly. They don't need little kids getting involved," her mother said. "You don't realize how dangerous criminals can be. This is no children's game."

"Have you discovered anything?" Shawn asked.

"That's not the point, Shawn," Polly's mom frowned.

Polly took a gulp of milk, to give herself a minute to think about what to say. She didn't want to cross her mom, but she didn't want to give up just when she and Kyle were getting close to some answers.

"We wouldn't do anything, Mom." Polly smoothed her jeans with nervous hands. "Kyle and I just think about stuff. We ask questions...like where did Rosalie DeCosta get a rabbit sketch? We make notes."

"Hey, if it isn't little Miss Encyclopedia Brown, or

Agatha Christie. I suppose Kyle the Clam is Sherlock Holmes." Shawn laughed out loud. "Give me a break."

"Have you figured anything out?" her dad asked.

"That's not the point, Ted," Polly's mom interrupted. "The point is she is a child and could get hurt."

Shawn stopped what he was doing and looked up, his brow furrowed, "She's not as little as you think, Mom."

"Besides, Thorn's being mean. Someone needs to figure out why," Polly said.

"I want you to promise to stop sticking your nose into other people's business." Polly's mom stood beside the table and waited for Polly to answer as the whistle of the kettle droned on.

"But we aren't doing anything dangerous," Polly protested.

"Promise?"

Polly's head bent close to her plate. "I promise." Then she raised her eyes. "Can I be excused? I have to walk George."

She reached in her pocket and tossed the information sheets about the two junior highs on the table.

"I'm trying to act responsibly," she said as she dashed for the door. Tears threatened to fall. "I'm not a little girl anymore, I'm in sixth grade." But she was already in the hallway as she muttered this last sentence.

What was the use? When her mom looked at her, she saw a little kid. "Maybe I really am invisible." She trudged down the corridor. "And I don't want to be, I don't want that at all."

Her brother Shawn came tumbling out the door carrying his hockey equipment. "So, tell me, kid, have you figured anything out?"

Polly glared at her brother. Ever since he'd gone to junior high and had been discovered as a hockey player, the two of them had gone their separate ways. Polly figured Shawn wanted it that way.

"Look, kid, I got thinking about what it was like when I was in sixth grade, you know. It's not easy." He shrugged his shoulders. "I don't think mom wants to lose her little kids. She can't see how big you are, because she doesn't want to." He stood there awkwardly, zipping and unzipping his jacket.

Polly brought him up to date on the investigation as the two of them walked towards the back door.

"Thorn was in Midget Hockey when I was in PeeWee. A good defenseman, tough. But he was a bully even then and picked on little squirts. Did you know Rudy is his uncle?" Shawn swung open the back door. "Seems to me Thorn went to jail for shoplifting."

"What do you think I should do?" Polly asked. "It's one thing to suspect someone, it's another to have proof. Someone's threatening Kyle. Kyle won't want to quit looking for answers. I don't want to quit either, but I promised."

"Well, you aren't really poking your nose into someone else's business, are you? It's your picture of a rabbit that Rosalie has." He sprinted off towards the bus stop. "If you need any help, let me know. It sounds to me like you and Kyle are getting close to some answers. That's why someone stole his stuff." He jogged away.

George barked from Isabel's balcony.

"No wonder Mom thinks I'm a dreamer...outside without George." Polly ran back inside to get the dog. At least one thing was safe. George, the dog, was a safe, cuddly friend who would trust her to the end of time.

9 Oh, No – Not George

GEORGE WAITED FOR HER AT THE DOOR OF ISABEL'S apartment. Polly snapped his leash to the bright blue collar with the metal dog tag and a silver disc showing he'd had his rabies shot. The two tags clinked together like old friends, or maybe like a brother and sister.

"Are you all right, Polly?"

Polly nodded.

"Seem quiet these days." Isabel sipped her after-dinner coffee. The news was on.

Polly clasped the heliotrope firmly. "Kyle and I are trying to figure out who the crooks are. Mom says we shouldn't stick our noses in other people's business. Shawn says he'll help."

"Don't do anything foolish," Isabel said.

"CITY POLICE ADVISE PEOPLE TO LOCK CAR DOORS," the radio announcer shouted. "AN UNPRECEDENTED WAVE OF ROBBERIES HAS TAKEN PLACE THIS HOLIDAY SEASON. DON'T LEAVE GIFTS OR PURCHASES ON AUTO SEATS. MAKE SURE APARTMENT DOORS, GARAGES, AND WINDOWS ARE SECURED."

Polly gulped.

"CALL 426-TIPS WITH ANY INFORMATION. REMEMBER THESE CRIMINALS MAY BE ARMED AND DANGEROUS."

Polly ran down the steps as the announcement finished. George tugged and wheezed, hastening for the outside door.

The winter darkness split wide open with street lights, porch lights, floodlit Christmas lawn ornaments. Strings of flickering red, blue, green, and yellow bulbs festooned trees and balconies. The distant sound of carols and the choir practising at the church floated high in the air. It didn't feel dangerous. But Polly, remembering her mother's warning and the radio announcement, walked along the busy, tree-lined street towards the park, instead of down the deserted laneway. George led her, stopping to sniff and circle every tree.

A black car pulled alongside. Polly yanked George's leash tight. The dog sat at attention beside her.

Detective Mills rolled down the window. "Didn't mean to startle you, Polly." The detective had on pearl earrings that dangled to her shoulders. She didn't look as severe as her voice sounded sometimes. Maybe she had to work at sounding old and businesslike.

Polly smiled. She was glad to see Detective Mills, because she would have had a hard time phoning the police station. She didn't really like phoning. She liked to see who she was talking to, watch their faces, see how they looked at her.

"We were wondering whether you and your friends had seen or heard anything else." Detective Mills got out and leaned against the car. George eyed her cautiously. "If the dog could talk, he'd be able to help," she said.

"Kyle found something." Polly told the detective about the list in the tree trunk and the missing dungeon and dragon books and figures. "Can you get fingerprints off the paper?"

"Why in the tree?" Detective Mills scratched her chin.

"I've been wondering if one crook phones to find an empty apartment and leaves a red tick by the name of the occupants – then puts the note back in the tree."

"That might work."

"Maybe we should put the list back in the tree and set up surveyors."

"You mean surveillance."

"Yeah, surveillance." Polly grinned thinking about Kyle and her on a stakeout.

"Next thing you know, you and Kyle will be signing up for police training," Detective Mills teased.

The phone in the squad car rang. George put his paws up on the door and peered in the window, fogging the glass with doggie breath. He woofed at the ringing and dropped down as Detective Mills opened the door.

"Thanks for the tip. We'll drop by and talk to Kyle as soon as we deal with this call." The detective picked up the phone, murmured a few words, then clutched the phone to her chest. "Be careful, Polly. Don't do anything on your own, okay?"

Polly raced George to the park as the car pulled away from the curb. There, she'd told the police all she knew. Now it was up to them. At least until she or Kyle figured out something more, and earned the title of Super Sleuths of Ninth Street. Maybe they'd get a reward from Crimestoppers. She could buy an artist's table and a high stool, just like Isabel's.

When she and George reached the park Polly unclipped the leash and let the dog loose. He ran in circles happily chasing his tail, then scampered into the bushes.

A small plane flew so low overhead Polly could see the passengers looking out little windows. Someday she'd fly over the clouds to faraway places. Not a country like Rosalie's and Arturo's where people weren't safe, where people couldn't trust each other. Unless the Invisible Polly McDoodle, the grownup, wanted to help others enough to risk her life. She wanted to help people but she didn't know how much. She could start small, start with little things for little people.

She would ask Rosalie if she wanted to come to the Christmas party at the church – Rosalie would get a Christmas present from Santa after the carol singing. First, Kyle and Polly had to talk to Arturo about a few things. If they could get him to trust them, that was.

George had calmed down. He snorted and sniffed, came over and sat in front of Polly, tail wagging.

"If you think I want to play fetch with you, George, you're nuts. It's too cold." However she got up, searched for a stick, and tossed it. A police siren wailed. One of the distinctive white and blue cars sped by.

"Like Detective Mills said, too bad you can't talk. You'd tell us all about the robbery." George stood in front of her, hesitating, the stick in his mouth, poised, ready to run. He dropped it by Polly's right toe.

Polly threw the stick several times, coaxing George to drop it when he came back, fake growling at her, his tail wagging like crazy. He was like a dumb little kid.

Polly laughed and ruffled his furry head, tickled his cold ears. The Fabulous McDoodle Dog Training Act.

She tossed the stick towards the bushes. It landed on the beaten path that crossed from one school yard to the other. The dog did a midair twirl and dashed off. He hunted in a circle for it, sniff, sniff, sniff.

"Dummy, it's right in front of your nose." Polly ran over. The dog was chewing something, licking his lips. He shook his head from side to side and walked away.

"Don't eat garbage, you'll puke." Polly clipped his leash on and pulled him homeward. "Enough, oh wild and woolly beast."

"Who are you talking to?" Kyle's voice startled Polly. He came strolling along the path, pushing his bicycle. "I just saw Detective Mills. She's pleased with our discoveries. Liked my map, too."

The two of them walked on, Kyle pushing the bike, George prancing between them.

"What have the Kims buried in their backyard?" Polly asked. "Maybe it's pot or hash or dope or something bad like that."

"Maybe they buried next year's bulbs."

"In a big crock?"

"I'm not too worried about them. We've known them for years. They make great candy apples." Kyle said. "I'm more worried about Arturo. We have to talk to him."

"We could ask him to join the fort." Polly drew in her breath. "He and Rosalie. Maybe if we asked him to join the fort he'd know we trusted him. I hate it that he told Rosalie not to talk to us."

Polly felt a sharp tug at the leash. George suddenly flopped down on the sidewalk in front of the apartment building. He rocked back and forth on his haunches but he didn't get up. He strained to stand but he couldn't get his body moving. His tail drooped. He turned his head toward Polly and his eyes looked like dark, glassy marbles.

"Come on, old buddy, you're nearly home. Don't poop out now." Polly squatted beside the dog. She felt blood rush to her head as she watched the dog's strange behaviour. She couldn't believe what was happening. George's legs stiffened and his eyes had gone wild. His nose was dry. Polly could feel her heart pounding in her chest as if it was trying to escape.

"Quick, Kyle, George is having a fit!"

Kyle had already taken off as if a ghost were after him.

"Oh, no, George! Oh, no boy...what's the matter?" Polly's head throbbed. The dog's eyes stared off in the distance, a drool of grass and white foam edging his clenched mouth. He lay quivering, heavy as a sack of potatoes. Polly wanted to run. She wanted to stay, holding the dog. "It's poison. You've been poisoned by the crooks – because you're a witness."

Isabel and Kyle came running down the walk. One glance, and Isabel lifted George and with Kyle's help carried the sick dog inside.

Kyle stayed with George in the vestibule while Isabel and Polly went inside to phone the emergency vet's number.

Two moments on the phone and Isabel's face looked drained of life. "She's afraid it's strychnine. We've got to hurry. It may be too late. What did he eat?"

Polly shook her head, ran and knocked on her own

door, stuck her head in, and yelled at her parents. She caught up to Isabel on the stairs.

"We'll save him," she said to Isabel, with more hope than confidence.

Isabel and Kyle loaded George in the back seat, his head propped on Polly's lap.

"Do up your seat belts," Isabel commanded.

The older woman wheeled out of the parking lot so fast gravel spit from the back tires like bullets.

Not a sound in the car. Kyle kept craning his neck, staring at George, still as a lump.

"He's still breathing." Polly's eyes filled with tears. God, please, don't let him die. Anger grew inside her chest. "Those crooks tried to poison the star witness," she sobbed.

Isabel glanced in the rear-view mirror. "I doubt it. How would the thieves know where to put the poison? Oodles of dogs and cats use that park."

"Could have put it in his dinner," Kyle said.

"I was home all afternoon," Isabel said. "Besides, the vet says poison works fast."

Polly moaned.

"It never rains but it pours." Isabel pulled into a parking space in front of the clinic. A young woman in a white lab coat hurried to meet them.

"Quick, put him on the examining table," she said.

Polly's arms shook as Kyle and Isabel lifted George from her lap. She gazed up into Kyle's eyes.

"Let me do this, Polly. I want to do this," Kyle said. His grip on George's body was as firm as his voice. Polly looked into Kyle's eyes and for just a moment she glimpsed an older boy, maybe even a hint of a man. She let go of George and let them carry the limp body.

Polly opened the door for them. Portraits of dogs, cats, and birds covered the walls. Kyle and Isabel disappeared with the vet through a dark green door. Polly paced the brown-tiled floor. Odours of disinfectant and dog shampoo filled the room. A brilliant green parrot with jingle bells on his cage cackled.

"Polly want a cracker?"

"How'd you know my name?" Polly asked. She let out a sigh as long as a thought.

The door to the examining room remained closed. Polly sat on one of the orange vinyl chairs lined against the wall.

"No, I don't want a cracker."

"Polly want a cracker?"

Polly lifted her downcast head and glared at the brightly coloured bird with its busy beak.

"So – you are a Polly too."

"Pretty Polly, pretty Polly, what a pet you are."

"Some pet."

"Polly want a cracker?" the bird chattered.

"Maybe that's it. Someone fed George crackers to keep him from barking while they robbed Isabel. That or dog biscuits. George loves dog biscuits. Kyle gives him sunflower seeds. Arturo gives him cookies. No wonder the dog's so fat."

"You're a pet, you are," the parrot said.

The door opened. Isabel and Kyle came out slowly. George wasn't with them. Polly stood up, her mouth open, afraid to ask anything, say anything, hope anything.

"They pumped his stomach." Isabel sat down, sighed

and took a hankie out of her purse.

"Wasn't strychnine." Kyle plopped on one of the orange chairs.

"How is he?" Polly whispered.

"She's keeping him overnight for observation." Isabel dabbed her eyes, put her hankie back in her purse, walked over and stared at the scrawny little Christmas tree – with dog and cat treats tied to it – standing in the corner of the waiting room. "I could lose my old friend."

"You're a pet, you are," the parrot screeched.

"Let's get out of here." Kyle pushed the door open, letting in a blast of cold air.

"It smells like snow." Isabel wrapped her coat around her, picked up her purse. The three of them walked to the car. Polly climbed in the front, Kyle in back.

Isabel inched onto the street and drove slowly home. Polly glanced over at her. Isabel's hands on the wheel were trembling, and a vein in her neck throbbed.

"He'll be fine, won't he?"

"I wish I had a dog," Kyle said. "Someone to talk to. Maybe if I had a dog like George to talk to...." He broke off.

Isabel braked for a red light.

"Kyle, if George gets better you can come visit him any time," Isabel said hoarsely. A tear rolled down her cheek. "You're great kids."

Polly bit her lip. Kyle traced circles in the ice on the side window.

"I think what you said back there will be a real help to the vet, Kyle." Isabel turned onto Ninth street. "I'm glad you spoke up."

Polly swung her head to watch Kyle drawing on the

window. She hadn't doodled a thing for hours. She hadn't had time. What had Kyle said? She wrinkled her forehead. Isabel, glimpsing her puzzled expression, filled her in.

"Kyle told the vet about the drug problem in the neighbourhood. How he suspects that kids are getting stuff in the park. The vet's going to run tests on George. He may have had an overdose. I'm sure glad you spoke up." Isabel nodded at Kyle.

Polly wagged her head from side to side in surprise. Imagine Kyle talking to a stranger like the vet. Imagine him knowing about drug dealing. This partner of hers had more secrets than the RCMP, as Robin would say.

Kyle shrugged his shoulders. "I thought it would help find an antidote if she knew what George had eaten."

Polly had seen strange teenagers and motorcyclists using their pocket park, but she had been more interested in drawing rabbits and trees than figuring out what they were doing there.

"When will the vet know...?" Polly hesitated.

"Tomorrow, if he's all right tomorrow...." Isabel's voice trailed off.

"The question is," Kyle traced the elusive rabbit on the steamy window. "The question is...does this have anything to do with the case, or is it a 'red herring'?"

"A red herring?" Polly shook her head. The car pulled into Isabel's parking spot.

"In many mysteries there is a false clue or two. Those are 'red herrings'."

"This isn't a book, dummy!" Polly shouted. "This is a dog, a real pet. A real pet that could die."

She burst into tears and ran for the door.

10 A Big Day for Everyone

POLLY WOKE WITH A START, THINKING ABOUT GEORGE, worried about the poor dog she'd taken for a walk. Her mouth felt dry as sandpaper. She lay there wondering if she dare wake her folks, tell them what a tough night she was having, tell them how bad she felt, like when she was a little kid with nightmares. She was a big kid now. Too big to bug her parents. She hugged herself tight, drew a big breath. Polly stretched out her toes, pulled the covers up to her chin, listened to the hum of early morning traffic, and drifted off to sleep again.

She dreamt of Isabel and George in a big white room. Isabel held out a big bowl of doggie treats, but every time George ran toward them, the bowl would shrink and disappear. Polly's arms ached from trying to reach into the room. She could see herself behind a thick pane of glass trying so hard to write notes to Isabel, to tell her what to do. The art paper pad was huge and cumbersome. The pencils left no mark. She started to cry, screaming so loud she woke herself.

Polly opened her eyes, sweating with the covers twisted around her and the top two buttons of her pajamas broken off. She got up, padded to the bathroom, came back and pulled on her pastel green track suit, tugged the hairbrush through her unruly red mop and tiptoed to the kitchen.

The clock said 7:00 a.m. The apartment was so quiet Polly could hear her heart pounding. She had to find out about George. She grasped the heliotrope rabbit, rubbing it between her fingers, willing the heaviness in the pit of her stomach to disappear. It was a feeling of being a complete and utter failure. She couldn't be trusted with keys, or dogs, or anything. Maybe her mom was right: maybe she was just a little kid.

She grabbed the camouflage coat, gloves, and toque, pulled them on, and stepped out onto the chilly balcony with its neatly covered barbeque, chained bikes, folded deck chairs, and box of empty flower pots. A string of multi-coloured lights taped to the iron railing flashed on and off, on and off. She stood silent, leaning on the railing, surveying the back lane. Isabel's car was gone.

What did that mean?

The elusive rabbit hopped down the lane to the willow, sat beneath its bare branches nibbling dead grass, alert, cautious, ears wiggling. All alone the rabbit was. Like Polly. Not invisible – neither one of them was invisible. They both had to stay alert, to listen, to be ready to move.

Thorn, his head covered with a huge floppy toque, wearing a dark coat, and carrying a full gym bag, appeared from between Polly's building and the Twins' house. What had he been doing so early in the morning?

At the sound of a car turning down the lane the

silence was broken, the rabbit stood up, turned her head both ways, and loped away through a hole in the Twins' fence. Thorn disappeared down the lane.

Isabel's car pulled in just as Polly's mom came jogging down the lane. Polly leaned out to wave and call, but thought better of it when she saw her mom approach the car.

"Any news?" Polly's mom did a leg stretch against the side of Isabel's car door. "About George?"

"I couldn't sleep so I drove over." Isabel's smile, visible even from the second floor, lit up the universe. Polly heaved a huge sigh. "George's going to be fine, probably sleep for a week. I can pick him up this afternoon. The vet says he's got a great constitution."

"I know Polly felt really sorry."

"Polly's like her mother," Isabel laughed. "Feels responsible for everything. Some things just happen. It was Kyle and Polly's quick-wittedness that saved George."

Polly's mom stopped mid-calf-stretch. "Funny you should talk about responsibility. Polly muttered the same thing last night as she went to get George. About being responsible."

"Kids in sixth grade are the best in my book," Isabel said. Polly strained every muscle to listen. "I loved teaching them. Of course, there's always a few turnips and toughies. But I loved watching them trying their wings, figuring out who they were. It's a very interesting age. Kids like Polly and Kyle – well, you can see what they are going to be like when they grow up, you can help them by being there for them. You can see the shadow of their grownup selves standing behind them.

I'm not saying this well. I just know I loved teaching them. It was a real treat."

Polly's mom jogged on the spot to keep warm. "I'm not too good with bigger kids. You can't control them and I'm a control freak. Ted's always after me about it. Babies – I liked babies. Polly was a fantastic baby."

Polly's mom bent to rescue a green card that banged against her leg in the sudden gust of wind. "Funny, it's a broken credit card, all chewed up along one edge. Must have fallen out of someone's garbage."

Polly thought about Shawn talking about crooks using credit cards when Detective Anderson stopped him. The *Journal* truck pulled in and dumped a pile of papers for early morning delivery. One of the university students collected them and strolled away with a *Journal* bag over his shoulder. She had a sudden picture of a canvas *Journal* bag – a *Journal* bag on the wrong shoulder, on the shoulder of someone who didn't have a *Journal* route. A bag that would be ideal for carrying small stolen items. Boy, standing here, invisible on the porch, she'd discovered more than all her hours of hunting for clues. She'd have to tell Kyle.

Isabel shivered in the cold breeze that swept across the parking lot. "I best let you go in, Jan. Sorry if I blathered on. Living alone, I guess. Being worried about George. Good to have neighbours." Isabel fetched a plastic bag with milk and bread from the front seat of her car.

"I'm staying home to do my Christmas baking today." Polly's mom and Isabel moved towards the doorway, out of Polly's vision. "Why don't you come for coffee at eleven, say? You could sample the shortbread."

Polly left the balcony and threw the jacket into the closet, darted into the bathroom and closed the door. She ran the shower, stepped into it, leaving her clothes in a heap on the floor.

George was okay. George was okay. Isabel loved kids in sixth grade. She was in sixth grade. She felt like going back to bed and having the sleep she missed, but it was Thursday and today was the concert. She and Kyle were going to talk to Arturo, see if they couldn't help. She figured she knew how the robberies had taken place. But where were all the stolen goods? Maybe they should talk to Detective Mills again.

"I'm dreaming of a White Christmas, just like the ones I used to know," Polly sang lustily.

"Shut up," her brother moaned from his room.

"Breakfast," Mom called.

BY THE TIME POLLY DRIED OFF, dressed, and blew her hair dry, the whole family had gathered at the table and were wolfing down bacon and eggs.

"It's a big day, eh, troops?" Dad flipped the lever on the toaster, driving four slices of brown bread in a shower onto the centre of the table. "I've been over setting up our Big, Before Christmas Midnight Madness Sales Event, your Mom's having a cooking fit, Shawn's got his big game." He paused to butter his toast. "And Polly's got criminals to chase, a concert, and one recovering dog to visit. Isabel doesn't think he'll be able to go for a walk for a few days."

"George is fine, Polly." Polly's mom left the cookie sheet she was greasing and came over behind Polly's chair, reached around and gave her a hug.

Polly could feel tears gathering, backing up behind her eyelids as if the whole of the North Saskatchewan River was dammed there. George's accident had made her kind of jumpy, like she didn't know where the next problem was going to come from.

Shawn winked at her, gathered his plate and glass, and moved to put them in the dishwasher. "Seems Isabel thinks you and Kyle saved George's life." He cleared his throat. "Acted quickly, acted responsibly."

Her mother was back in the kitchen, stirring peanut butter clusters. Her dad loaded the dishwasher. For a minute or two the room was silent. Polly sat shoving her egg away from her bacon. She couldn't think of anything to say. Indeed, she was afraid she would cry if she opened her mouth. She could hear Kyle practicing upstairs. The sound of music floating through the walls made her feel good. She hoped that finding his voice wouldn't mean that Kyle would stop playing.

"We don't want you getting hurt," her mother said brusquely.

"We want you to be careful," her dad said.

"I guess what we are trying to say," her mother stammered, "is that we're proud of you."

"We get busy," her dad said.

"Preoccupied," her mother added.

"It's okay." Her dad turned and looked her full in the face.

Polly's arms felt heavy but she made herself walk over to her dad and give him a hug. Her mom joined them.

"I was so worried about George, about Isabel," she sobbed into her dad's shirt, her mother's blouse.

"Listen, kid, have a good cry," her dad said. "Families have a tough time at Christmas keeping their priorities straight."

"Honey, you and Kyle keep on with your investigation. Just tell us, okay? We'll help." Her mom danced around the room. "Maybe there's a course for struggling young detectives I could sign you up for." The McDougalls laughed together.

"Go get ready for school," her dad said. "Enough of this malipalaver, as one cowpoke said to the other."

"Could you run over to Safeway and get me more butter for my shortbread?" Her mother was greasing cookie sheets.

"Sure," Polly dipped one finger into the cookie batter and stuck it in her mouth, licking, tasting, savouring its peanutty, sugary flavours.

The two information sheets about junior highs were tacked to the refrigerator door − side by side. Polly stared at them. Her mother stood looking at them, shaking her head.

"I don't like the idea of you taking two buses to get to Kirby. It's a long way," her mother said. "Who knows what kind of people you'd run into, what things you'd leave on the bus...?"

Her mother was still talking as Polly left the kitchen.

11. Polly Pursues the Truth

BACK IN HER ROOM POLLY PICKED UP HER SKETCH book and flipped through the past week's work. She studied her sketch of Arturo with a *Journal* bag, the full page drawing of the old beat-up car with its Montana licence plates, a side by side sketch of Spiker, the punk, doing dishes and Spiker the ordinary person.

Polly stared at Spiker. Maybe Spiker wore all that make-up and hair colour so she wouldn't be invisible. Without all the goop she looked okay, not spectacular, but okay.

And Thorn, what about Thorn? Without his purple braids and earrings, what would he look like? Polly grabbed her pencil and started sketching, whistling "Frosty the Snowman" under her breath. Drawing made some of her worries fade.

"Polly, are you asleep at the switch in there?" her dad hollered. "Mom needs you."

Polly dashed from her room, dropped her knapsack by the front door, and reported for the shopping list and money.

"I need two more pounds of butter, baking powder,

and raisins." Her mom handed her a twenty-dollar bill.

"Don't put any raisins in my cookies," Shawn shouted from the bathroom over the sound of his blow dryer.

"Your brother has selective ears. He only hears what he wants to," Mom laughed. "Hurry now."

Only three other shoppers hurried down the aisles of the giant Safeway. The terrazzo floors echoed under Polly's running feet as she wheeled her cart up and down looking for raisins. No one else was at the check-out counter. The mall loudspeaker announced the Midnight Madness Sale. The checkout woman ran out of machine tape and disappeared. Polly stared out the window at the nearly deserted parking lot.

She blinked twice, leaned her head to the left to see through the tinted plate glass windows, past a huge cardboard Frosty the Snowman and the Foodbank shelves, just as Thorn's van pulled into a parking spot by the Pancake House. Two cold looking skinny kids in worn leather jackets, one carrying a heavy gym bag, the other with a *Journal* sack weighing down his right shoulder, strolled over to Thorn.

Thorn grabbed the bags from the kids, swung open the back door of the van and emptied the contents of each bag. He reached in, running his hands through the stuff, handed the kids each something, slammed the door, locked it and walked with them into the restaurant.

The checkout woman returned and apologized for the delay. Polly nodded, grabbed the grocery bag, and ran out the door. She bolted for the van, darting glances to the right and left, back in the direction of the restaurant, then climbed quickly onto the back bumper of the van, holding herself tight to the door by clinging to the chrome ladder. She took one mitten off to clean the dirty window, shielded her eyes from the glare of the morning sun and stared into the van.

At first she couldn't see a thing, but as her eyes adjusted to the dark interior she spotted several discarded *Journal* bags laying in a heap behind the driver's seat. A row of brown boxes lined the wall, most of them closed. The box closest to the door lay open. An Eaton's bag, an Excelsports bag, and several smaller Christmas-wrapped gifts tumbled together in confusion.

"Hey, what are you doing?" A shout startled Polly. She dropped to the ground, picked up the bag of groceries and lit out towards her back lane, the sound of running feet behind echoing in her ears. She risked a glance over her shoulder. Thorn and the two kids ran after her. To her left a stream of oncoming cars headed down Kingsway. Polly gulped and dashed across in front of the heavy morning traffic.

"Hold it right there!" Thorn shouted, caught on the mall side of the six-lane expressway. Polly loped home, huffing and puffing. Billows of cold air from her breath surrounded her head.

A police cruiser sat parked by the garbage tins near the apartment building. Detective Mills stepped out as Polly ran for the door.

"What's up, Polly?"

Polly told her. The police cruiser pulled away, blocking the lane from the expressway. "Don't worry, Polly, we'll just ask Mr. Thorn a few questions. Now's a good time for you to make yourself scarce. It's police business."

Kyle came down the stairs at a gallop as Polly lugged in the groceries.

She opened the door, handed her mother the bag, and grabbed her knapsack.

"You're out of breath," her mother commented." Is everything okay?"

Polly nodded, motioned to Kyle, and the two of them skipped down the steps. At the door Polly put a finger to her lips, peered down the lane towards the mall, then down the lane towards the school. Quickly she brought him up to date on everything.

"All clear," she said. "Detective Mills says we should leave it up to them now." Her breath still came in little gasps. "We've got one more thing to sort out, no matter what Detective Mills says."

"Where's the goods?" Kyle whispered. "Detective Anderson said thieves have to sell the stuff they take. Some stuff they sell to pawn shops and secondhand dealers. Some they send to another city where it can't be traced."

The Kims's cat ran across the lane. No sound came from Rudy's garage or backyard.

"Where's Chief?" Polly pointed to the junky yard where the German shepherd usually sat.

"Out in Rudy's truck?" Kyle nodded toward the empty spot where the 4 by 4 was usually parked.

"I'd sure like to know what goes on in there." Polly walked over to the metal frame building.

Kyle pointed up to a dirty window about six feet off the ground. A gray army blanket partially covered the inside.

"What are you two up to?

Kyle and Polly jumped.

Shawn came down the lane towards them, swinging

his hockey bag. He stopped beside them, dropped his bag and grabbed Polly by the waist.

"Upsadaisy, baby," Shawn groaned. "Boy, are you heavy. What ever happened to my little sister?"

Once again Polly found herself wiping a dirty window with a now dirty mitt.

"Well?" Kyle said.

"Whumpf," Shawn moaned. "Hurry up."

"I see the old car. It's been all fixed up, repainted, sitting on the blue trailer with its trunk open."

"So? Rudy fixes cars, we know that," Shawn said.

Polly stared for another couple of minutes, taking in the crisp freshly painted smooth auto body, the shiny licence plates with blue and white numbers, WIZ230. A giant blue tarp lay folded on the top of the car. Piles of cardboard boxes sat on the floor. Some were loaded in the trunk. A battered suitcase lay on its side, with a pair of fishing boots and a slicker.

"Enough!" Her brother crouched and Polly slipped off.

The warning bell rang at the school.

"Thanks, Shawn." Polly and Kyle bolted towards the school yard. Shawn retrieved his hockey bag and headed for the arena and his last practice.

As they ran Polly and Kyle discussed the *Journal* bag, the stuff in the van, the broken credit card, and what Polly had seen inside Rudy's Body Shop. When she slipped into her desk she pulled out the sketch book from her knapsack and quickly drew a picture of everything she remembered from Rudy's, then flipped back to check something out about the old car. Jones stood talking to the principal at the classroom door, so Polly had time to sketch Thorn and the two kids, then finish the drawing of Thorn without his purple hair and weird clothes.

Robin poked her on the shoulder, "Arturo met Kyle and me outside Isabel's door. He was worried about the dog, you know. He likes him as much as we do. I told him we wanted to be friends. He still seems worried but we set something up." Robin handed Polly a note. *TC2 interview with Arturo at recess. K.*

"Polly, what do you have there?" Jonesy stood so close to her desk Polly could smell his after shave.

She gulped and opened her sketch book, sliding Kyle's note between two pages, meanwhile laying the book open showing the bird's eye view of the lane.

"Interesting, but I want to see the note, Polly," the teacher said.

She gave it to him and leaned back in her chair, waiting for the explosion. Mr. Jones stood in the aisle reading the note. He read it twice, scratching his head.

"Kyle, I believe this is your property. I see you are as voluble in writing as you are in speech. Not very. A code name, even. Well, well! Too bad you two aren't throwing all this natural creativity into your work these days."

The other kids in the class laughed.

"Seriously, children, I don't want you getting hurt." Jonesy tapped his foot, tore the note up and threw it in the wastebasket. "Good thing for you tomorrow is the last day of school before Christmas break. I haven't time for the invisible life of kids. Tonight's the concert. Robin, Kyle, and Polly can help set up chairs during recess instead of going outside."

Polly, Kyle, and Robin ducked their heads, glanced at each other from behind bushy eyebrows and kept quiet.

Arturo, sitting at the front of the class, looked around. His eyes were huge and sad as ever.

The meeting with Arturo would have to wait for lunchtime.

The elusive rabbit smiled from the corner of Polly's sheet of math problems. She grabbed her eraser and rubbed, watching the doodle disappear. Jonesy didn't mind her doodling, just not on worksheets. Polly smiled back at the rabbit.

I think I know how the crooks did the robberies, but I don't know where Isabel's jewels are. Polly slid a spare piece of paper out of her desk. She drew the tree fort with all its members, old and new, and signed it, *The TC2, Christmas Week, by PMcD.*

ROSALIE STOOD SHIVERING in the school yard at lunchtime, waiting for her brother. Kyle, Polly and Robin hurried toward her. Arturo hung back behind Kyle, his eyes furtive, darting from one kid to the other.

"Let's head to the fort," Robin said cheerily.

"What's going on?" Rosalie asked.

"We are inviting you and your brother to become members of the House of the Elusive Rabbit," Polly blurted. "I know you've seen the rabbit."

Arturo moved slower and slower, kicking pebbles as the troop hurried down the lane.

"*Paré!* Stop!" he shouted. "It is impossible. If you knew...."

Kyle dropped back and banged the slender boy on the arm. He shrugged his shoulders and pointed to Thorn's house.

Arturo stood stock still in the centre of the laneway. He glanced up and down, over towards Thorn's, then at Rudy's. He reached into his gym bag and drew out a long thin parcel. Without saying a word he handed the package to Robin, then backed away as if to run. Kyle held his arm. "We know."

Robin took the skinny package and unrolled it while Arturo averted his eyes. Rosalie huddled close to Polly, her eyes fixed on Robin. "I think you don't want us."

"My recorder!" Robin shouted. "It's my recorder. Where did you find it?"

Arturo tried to pull away from Kyle but Kyle held tight.

Polly stood beneath the arms of the old willow. "We know, Arturo. You can trust us."

Arturo shook his head. "I am the thief."

"You're the thief?" Robin clutched her recorder to her chest. "What do you mean? Did I miss something again?"

"He means he helped Thorn get into your place. The real thief is Thorn, not Arturo," Polly said grimly. "Thorn had a key to the outside door he never handed in. He used a credit card to open the inside apartment doors. He had Arturo phone ahead and then leave a message in the tree. I was curious about why he had been up and down the laneway so often lately."

"I saw him downstairs by the laundry room a couple of days ago," Robin admitted.

"That fits," Polly nodded. "He may have stashed things in the laundry room when he needed to walk out without anything in his hands. I've seen him with a gym bag."

Kyle came and stood beside Polly under the willow

tree. He motioned for Arturo and Rosalie to join them. "Arturo was intimidated."

"What?" Robin frowned.

"Thorn tried to intimidate me." Kyle pried his mouth open like it was a can of spaghetti. "He tried to get me to give him keys to the apartments. He'd heard my dad had the masters."

"You didn't give them to him, did you?" Robin asked.

"No, I didn't. He shook me and tried rattling my teeth, but I didn't."

Arturo looked away, eyes blinking.

"Look, Arturo, I've lived here all my life. I don't come from a country where life is dangerous."

"What did Thorn say, Arturo? How did he threaten you?" Polly asked. She wanted to reach out and touch the boy's hand, tell him it was going to be all right. Instead she gave Rosalie a hug and felt the younger girl's thin body shiver.

He'd been silent so long, suffering, thought Polly, he can't talk. Maybe he, too, felt invisible.

"Tell them, Arturo," Rosalie said. "These are friends."

"He said he would have us deported." Arturo choked on his words as if they were broken glass. "He said he knew people in Ottawa that would say my father was a criminal and my mother was in no danger at home. So Papa could not join us, and Mama and Rosalie and I would have to go back."

"And you believed him?" Robin asked. "You believed that punk?"

Arturo nodded his head sadly. "He told me to trust no one, especially you kids. He said he had heard you laughing at me. He said I had no friends in this country but him. He gave me a *Journal* bag to carry the stuff away."

"The daytime robberies he must have done by himself, while you were at school." Polly chewed her lip.

"I expect he does the same thing with those other kids you told me about," Kyle said. "He's like a little Fagin, the guy in *Oliver*, intimidating kids, getting keys to apartment buildings, trading the stuff for money. It's quite an operation."

"Does he have a key to all the apartments around here?" Robin asked.

"Anywhere some kid lets him in. He intimidated them, too," Kyle said.

"The couple I saw this morning seemed pretty mean. I wouldn't want to run into them again."

"Some kids are mean," Kyle sighed.

"Arturo's not mean," Rosalie said.

"We know that," Polly patted Arturo on the back with her left hand. "Why didn't you tell your mother?"

"My mother is too busy learning the language, working at the hospital, worrying about Papa, and the rest of the family. I didn't want to worry her more." He hung his head. "Now she will be very hurt. I have hurt her."

Polly thumped her mitts together. "This meeting of the House of the Elusive Rabbit is called to order," she grinned. "I nominate Arturo and Rosalie DeCosta as full-fledged members. Have you seen the rabbit?"

"Oh, yes," Rosalie giggled. "It ate a carrot I left for it in the park."

"I saw it when I hid the phone list," Arturo confessed.

The group of kids chattered under the tree, planning their next move.

"Polly, kids, time for lunch!" Her mother stood on the balcony, flour to the elbows, smudge of flour on her cheek, a floury apron. Gorgeous smells of shortbread, peanut butter cookies, and cinnamon somethings came wafting to the willow tree.

"TC2, meet here after and we'll walk back to school together, just in case the police haven't caught the real crooks yet," Polly said.

"Tonight's the show and the showdown," Kyle offered.

12. A Fight

A POLICE SQUAD CAR WAS PARKED ON NINTH IN FRONT of Thorn's later that afternoon, as Polly and Robin headed home from school across the park. Until they saw it, they had been talking about their plans for going to the concert. Robin kept doing a dance step that she was unsure of. For a little while it was good to forget about the series of robberies and concentrate on the rest of life.

Polly felt her body go on alert when she saw the car. She studied the neighbourhood quickly. Two uniformed officers stood inside Thorn's opened garage. A plain-clothes detective had his head in the garbage can. Brutus, the springer spaniel, sniffed at the guy's ankles.

Rudy, his dog, and his truck with the blue trailer were pulling out, turning the corner. The refinished car was hidden under a bright blue tarp. Only the licence plate showed, and Polly knew it had changed. Rudy glanced in the direction of Thorn's and sped away.

Polly motioned with her hand for Robin to stop. "They brought the car from Montana. Now it's got BC licence plates. I bet they stole it."

"I've got my recorder back. I have to finish packing,"

Robin protested. "I hope they find our tickets, though. I don't think you and Kyle should be doing all this investigating. Thorn could get mean. I wish you'd stop it. It makes me nervous."

"Do the police know Rudy is Thorn's uncle?" Polly talked on, ignoring Robin's protests. She tiptoed across the frozen brown grass towards Thorn's. The police car pulled into the traffic on Ninth. Just then the two skinny kids she'd seen that morning came out of the bushes in the pocket park. They walked briskly towards Polly and Robin.

"You two girls don't want to go home," one sneered.

"Not yet, anyway." The second one was swinging a baseball bat and giggling in a funny voice. "Maybe you should play ball with us."

"We could use rocks for the ball," said the taller kid. "Or your heads."

"Try to catch rocks." The second guy giggled again.

The police car sped down the lane from the other end and turned down the side street by the park. Polly broke past the two bullies, pulling Robin with her. She frantically waved at the police.

The two kids didn't see the police car but made another grab for Polly and Robin, pinning them both to the ground. Polly stared into the eyes of the wiry kid holding her down.

"You've got a big mouth, Polly McDougall. It's time someone pasted it shut," he shouted.

The cords of his neck were tight as tied ropes, and his breath on her face was as sour as old socks. Beads of sweat rimmed his eyebrows. His face was red, nearly purple. Time froze. Polly could feel the cold hard ground beneath her, hear Robin screeching. Words were jammed in Polly's throat but she couldn't dislodge them. The kid was strong, his hands held her wrists to the icy grass. The two of them were locked together.

Through the haze of pain and panic her inner voice screamed, if he lets go of one hand you can hit him. Since he was sitting on her stomach, her breath had deserted her. Her throat hurt. The kid had to let go if he was going to hit her.

"So go ahead – hit me, stupid!" she taunted. He let go of her left hand, a flash of anger in his eye. Polly whomped him on the side of the head with her released fist. "What's that big bully Thorn got on you, eh?"

Whumpf! He punched her jaw.

"Okay, you guys, quit it!" Footsteps thudded over the frozen school yard. As a young police officer approached, the kids in black jackets ran towards the hospital grounds. The officer hesitated, looking down at Robin and Polly and then at the running figures.

"Are you kids okay?" he asked. "Maybe I should go after them...."

The exhaled frosty breath of Robin, Polly, and the police officer hung in the air like a small cumulus cloud.

"It's too late," Polly said. "We're all right." Robin nodded, massaging the back of her head. The two girls followed the police officer over to the cruiser.

"Did you arrest Thorn?" Polly asked when they reached the car. "He's the ringleader, you know. He's making kids help him."

The police officer with them glanced at the one sitting behind the wheel. Neither said anything. Their car radio squawked.

"Those two kids are members of his gang," Polly wheezed. "I saw them with him this morning.... Where's Detective Mills?"

Robin was tugging at her sleeve. "Leave it to them, okay, Polly? I'm scared."

Detective Mills appeared at Polly's shoulder. "If you kids would go home, Officer Connelly and I could keep Thorn under surveillance."

"Did you find Isabel's stuff?" Polly asked. "Have you checked Rudy's place?"

"Our airline tickets?"

Detective Mills gave the two girls a polite shove towards the lane and walked over to a dark car hidden behind a clump of caragana hedge. "Let us handle it, Polly. We don't want you getting hurt. It's one thing to play detective, and quite another to find evidence and capture criminals."

Polly kicked a stone so it crashed against Rudy's fence. She was still upset by the fight. Everything seemed to be happening at once. Now that the whole story of the crime was coming together and she wanted to be included, Detective Mills had become as cagey as the crooks. Polly itched to tell the detective all the stuff she and Kyle had figured out. She was excited.

It gave her a funny feeling, a feeling Polly couldn't ever remember having before − like she was a real person, not some little kid. But none of the big people knew it yet. She'd have to think more about that. The fingers in her pocket wiggled, wanting to doodle, doodle and think.

"What's the matter with you?" Robin asked. "I'm glad I'm going away. Every time I hang out with you we get into trouble. My head hurts and I can't even tell my folks or they'll blow a gasket. It's a good thing I didn't hurt an ankle or something. I have to dance."

Polly shook her head and ran up the steps to her apartment. Some things even close friends can't help with. Some things you have to work out by yourself. She felt glad about some things, mad about others: mad at the police, mad at Detective Mills. Couldn't anyone see the real Polly, the changing, growing Polly?

Shawn hollered as she came through the door. "Here's the intrepid detective, home from another daring adventure."

"Oh, shut up." Polly threw her coat in the closet.

"You look like you've been in a fight."

"Mind your own business!" Polly yelled.

"Merry Christmas to you, too." Shawn raised his arms in a gesture of defeat, and turned back to cooking himself steak and onions. He had the radio on full blast, roaring the sports scores.

Polly grabbed a handful of shortbread cookies and stuffed one in her mouth to keep from saying something mean to him. After all, he had helped her look in Rudy's window. Not that she'd had time to tell Detective Mills what she thought, or that she figured the police should be chasing Rudy's truck as it sped away, instead of digging through the punk's garbage. Who was going to listen? She had a shower, put on her good clothes, and came out to grab a bite of supper. A pile of uncooked hamburgers sat on the counter.

Polly's mom and dad came bounding out of their room dressed for the hockey game, beaming and talking to each other. Polly's dad started cooking hamburgers.

"I don't see why you have to go back to the store tonight. We'd promised Shawn our wholehearted attention." Her mom walked right past Polly like she wasn't there.

"It's this Midnight Madness Sale," Dad said. "None of my troops are seasoned enough to take advantage of people in a buying mood just before Christmas."

"I thought we were taking Shawn out for treats."

"Well, the two of you could come over to the mall. I could take a few minutes off."

"Ted, I wish you'd told me sooner." Mom plugged in the kettle for tea. "You're too easy-going. I like things organized, you know that. You change plans just to get my goat."

Shawn ate his steak in silence. Polly stood listening to her folks nattering. She reached up and touched the heliotrope encircling her neck, thinking she didn't need a heliotrope, not to be invisible to her folks, not to be dismissed by the police, not to be left sorting things out by herself. Except for Kyle and Isabel, she really didn't have anyone. Kyle understood. Polly could feel a tide rising in her, like the North Saskatchewan when it poured rain.

"Excuse me for living!" she cried. "I'm going to check on George and Isabel. Let you folks get on with more important things – like hockey heroes, and Midnight Madness!"

Polly hauled her jacket from the closet and ran to the door. "Isabel's coming to the school concert. Maybe she'll take me out for a treat at the mall afterwards. Don't wait up."

Polly moved to the stairwell and leaned hidden there,

her chest heaving like she'd lifted a refrigerator, wondering what had made her so angry, waiting for someone to come to the McDougall apartment door. Her mother appeared, glanced up and down. "She's gone, Ted."

A voice inside the apartment mumbled something Polly couldn't hear. There was another mumble.

"I know it's not easy being the younger. No, it's not easy being a girl. It's Christmas and she's excited. She's so touchy, though."

Mumble, mumble.

"She has to learn to share the spotlight." Polly's mother closed the apartment door.

Polly turned and looked down the hall towards Isabel's apartment. She could walk George, go to the concert, or...she stared at her own door, solid 201 with its Christmas wreath, the red bow needing to be retied, a piece of tinsel blowing in the current from the ceiling fan.

Polly gulped, straightened her shoulders and opened the door. Her mom and dad were sitting at the kitchen table. Dad had his hamburger halfway to his mouth. Mom was cutting hers neatly in half. Shawn was whistling in the bathroom, the water running.

"I came back."

No one said anything.

"I want to say something."

Their faces seemed frozen, expectant. Her father put down his hamburger and cocked his head. Her mother had stopped cutting her food and was staring at her, hard.

Polly could hear her heart beating as if it was behind her ears.

"You said I need to learn to share the spotlight. I don't think I've ever been in the spotlight. I've been invisible. But I want you to know something about me – that's why I came back. I'm not a little kid any more. I'm a big kid. I've got decisions to make about where to go to school, how to help people I like, how to become really good at art. I don't like being ignored at home. I want people to talk to about important stuff. I count for something. I can help solve crimes and take on bullies but I can't make you guys listen to me. I'm more invisible than the rabbit in a park full of snow." Polly could feel tears gathering. "I get lonely sometimes. I get...."

"Polly," her father lifted up his hand, stopping her in mid-sentence.

Her mom had grabbed the edge of the table with both hands. Her face had turned red. Polly trembled as her mother's eyes scanned Polly's face as if she was a complete stranger. "You've been saving this speech for some time, I gather." Her voice was flat. "Are you saying we are bad parents? Is that what you are saying, Polly?"

Polly shook her head.

"Jan, wait a minute." Polly's dad took the hand he had been reaching toward Polly and rested it on his wife's arm. He combed the fingers of his other hand through his salt and pepper curls. "We need to think about this before we say anything." He looked at Polly's mom, his lips pressed together. "We could have a special family meeting tomorrow to talk about things. I don't have to go to work and neither does your mom."

Polly's mom shuddered as if someone had walked on her grave, and with some effort pulled her hands away from the table and stood up. She walked over to Polly slowly, patted her on the shoulder, her fingers hesitating.

"Go to Isabel's."

Waves of anger seemed to be rocketing around the room.

"Is that okay with you, small fry?" Her dad looked sheepish suddenly. "I mean, Polly."

Polly nodded. She had no words left. She tugged her mitts on and headed out the door again. In her head splashes of red, yellow, and black like flames leapt and swirled.

She didn't want to be invisible anymore. She would give Isabel back the heliotrope tonight.

13. The Concert

GEORGE DIDN'T GREET POLLY AT THE DOOR. HE WAS lying in state on a brand new doggie bed, a round fat doughnut pillow of bright red with a smaller red pillow tucked inside. His eyes flickered and he moaned a hello. His tail wagged. He tried to pull himself up but his rump wouldn't work. Instead Polly curled up beside him. He had rotten doggie breath but he was alive.

Isabel stood combing her hair. "I'm nearly ready. Kyle's coming. You're quiet."

"I just blew up at my folks."

"Oh," Isabel said.

She brought Isabel up to date on the morning's escapade with Thorn, the attack in the park, the things she had said to her parents.

"Do you think my mom and dad will hate me now?"

Isabel didn't say anything.

"I couldn't help myself."

"Sometimes it's good to clear the air."

"I love my mom and dad."

"I know."

What Polly couldn't say out loud even to Isabel, what

she could only whisper to herself in her head was the really big question – can I say stuff like I said and still go home? Will anyone want me?

The doorbell rang.

"Ready?" Kyle asked. His silent parents stood behind him in their tweed coats, black berets, country walking boots.

"I forgot to eat," Polly said as her stomach rumbled. "All I had was three shortbread cookies."

Isabel grabbed an apple from the bowl in the middle of her kitchen table. "Here, eat this. We'll go out later."

They trooped down to the Clays' old green Volvo station wagon.

The Weinsteins were pulling out of their parking spot. Rosalie and her mother walked arm in arm down the lane.

"Where's Arturo?" Polly rolled down the window and asked.

"He's coming in a few minutes. Says he has one last delivery to make," Rosalie said.

Kyle nudged Polly. "He told me he was going to take everything, all the things Thorn had given him, drop them off in the old *Journal* bag by Thorn's back stoop."

"Isn't that dangerous?" Polly asked. "What if the police catch him."

Kyle limbered his fingers for his concert number. He shrugged his shoulders.

POLLY SAT IN THE THIRD ROW from the front with the grade four to six choir. The gymnasium was filled with the noise of parents talking, chairs creaking, feet clumping, and whispers everywhere, kids to kids, teachers to teachers, parents to neighbours. At the far side of the hall Isabel Ashton perched on her chair, back straight, wrapped in her brown shawl. Mr. Jones stood beside her chattering away. They must know each other. People in Polly's life kept making connections, some good ones and some not so good. This one was great.

Mrs. Stock, the third grade teacher, rushed up with some sugarplum fairies in tow. "Rosalie is so worried about her brother she won't put on her tin soldier costume."

Polly left her program on her chair and went backstage. A tearful Rosalie stood talking to her mother.

"Polly, oh, Polly, where's Arturo? Did you see my brother?"

Just then a red-faced Arturo rushed through the back door of the gym, gave his mother a small hug, patted his sister's arm, and followed Polly to the choir. He pressed a note in her hand before he slipped into a seat in the row behind her, right beside Kyle.

Polly unfolded the note and read it. *TC2. T & s plan escape. Police after me.* Polly refolded the note and passed it to Kyle, nodding at Arturo, trying to look encouraging. Craning her neck once more, she could see the two uniformed police officers she had seen at Thorn's that afternoon. They were standing with their backs to the wall, their eyes on Arturo.

If only they would give her a chance to explain everything, they'd understand why Arturo had gone with Thorn into the apartments, called ahead for him, even hung onto the small "gifts" Thorn had given him from each robbery. Did they put boys of twelve in jail?

The principal called for everyone's attention. They sang the National Anthem. Polly pushed all the worries and excitement out of her head to make room for the school concert. She could hear Kyle cracking his knuckles, chewing sunflower seeds. Silly kid, didn't he know how good he was on that dumb piano?

The curtains opened and the kindergarten band and choir came marching on. Wow! What tiny little things they were. Imagine, she and Kyle had looked like that seven years ago. Now they were gearing up to leave Central and go to junior high. Her mind flew towards the future, dreaming, not listening to the music, not paying attention to anything in the room. A crash of cymbals, drums, and ten triangles brought her back to the present. She focused her attention on the stage, the crowd clapping as the children marched off behind the little drummer boy. For some reason, Polly looked over at the side door. And who was sneaking in, slipping into seats behind Isabel? It was her parents! Polly looked at her watch and then back at her parents. What were they doing here? What about Shawn's game?

Bubbles of happiness foamed like soapsuds. Her parents had come after all. Did that mean they weren't too mad at her?

The stage lights turned blue for the dancers with Robin Weinstein in their midst. Polly watched the girls come on gracefully, walking like they were woodland fairies. Her mom would like this number for sure – if Polly had been like Robin her mother would be cheering.

Her eyes lifted to take in the full effect of the backdrops, the three-part mural she and the two artists from

Mrs. Begley's sixth grade had designed and made. She sighed with relief. They looked great. One panel carried the map of the world with stars pointing to where each kid or their parents came from. The centre panel had Jesus, Mary, and Joseph because Christmas was named for Jesus' birthday. The last panel held a giant snowman with kids of all colours helping build it, made of hundreds of wads of cotton batten. Polly had glue and cotton batten stuck on everything she wore to school that week. Polly rubbed her fingers, scratching where a few gummy flecks had resisted the scrub brush.

Kyle cleared his throat twice. He was running his long fingers through his straw-coloured hair, making it stand out like porcupine quills. He stood and slid past Arturo and two other kids. As he passed, Polly gave him an A-okay, you'll-do-great sign with her hand. Her glance toured the audience again, checked out the police at the back, her parents, Isabel and Jonesy sitting side by side.

The kid beside her poked her in the ribs. "We're next, flake."

Polly faced the front, listened to the applause for Kyle Clay, listened to his music float to the gym rafters, making rainbow colours flow in her head. Too bad about his hair and his dumb red sweater, but oh, well, you can't have everything. Some day she'd take him aside and talk to him about not sticking out like a sore thumb.

The choir stood during the applause and made their way to the stage. Polly waved her hand just a little, down by her side, as the choir filed past her mom and dad, to let them know she saw them, that she was glad they were there. Mrs. DeCosta was sitting with them. The Clays sat beside her, solid, quiet, looking nearly as old as Isabel. Funny kind of parents they'd be, like living in a library. Did they ever talk? No wonder Kyle was such a clam.

Isabel was grinning, gesturing with her head towards the backdrops, nodding her approval. She liked them. That was great. If only Polly could find those precious stones, if they hadn't already been sold or pawned or carried away by Rudy.

She climbed to the stage and stood beside her class-mates, singing her part loud and clear, singing in harmony the alto notes, the same notes as Kyle and Arturo. The choir voices blended.

"I'd like to teach the world to sing in perfect harmony." Please, Polly wished as she sang, let everything work out before Christmas, let Arturo be okay, and Isabel, and dumb old me, Polly McDoodle.

She reached for the heliotrope and brought it out to rest on her white blouse. Brightly coloured, flashing in the floodlights. Not so invisible as all that, eh, rabbit? Elusive, maybe, just like you. My art work is on the stage, my voice is in the choir, my family is in the audi-ence. Not bad for starters.

"We wish you a Merry Christmas, we wish you a Merry Christmas," the choir sang. The audience clapped. The lights came up.

"Polly, that was terrific," her mother said. "Now, I've got to run back to the arena to catch the third period. Your dad is staying with you."

Dad cleared his throat. "We wanted you to know something. We want you to know...."

Mom stopped, kissed the top of Polly's red head. "Oh, yes, We're proud of you, your backdrops – your art work is very good. Especially behind the dancers. Looked good behind the dancers, didn't you think?" Then her mom was gone.

Her dad had his arm around her shoulder. Arturo and his sister and mother stood beside the Clays, Isabel, and Mr. Jones.

"Instead of going downstairs for coffee, why don't we go over to the mall for ice cream?" Dad said. "This calls for a celebration."

The two police officers were making their way towards Arturo. Polly whispered in her dad's ear. "Don't let them take him away."

Kyle had been talking to his dad too. Mr. Clay joined the DeCostas, stuffing his beret in his pocket.

"Arturo DeCosta," the police officer said, adding his name and rattling off a bunch of serious stuff. Then he said, "I'd like to ask you to come with us to the police station to answer some questions."

"I'm Arturo's lawyer," Mr. Clay said briskly, nodding at Mrs. DeCosta. "His mother and I will come with him."

"I'm afraid Arturo has been involved in criminal activity. We have evidence that he is a member of a gang of juvenile thieves."

"But he was intimidated!" Polly shouted. Kyle laid his hand on her arm.

"Sshh," he said. "Leave it to my dad. He'll look after Arturo, believe me."

Mrs. DeCosta grabbed her son in her arms. She started talking quickly in Spanish, crying.

"Mama, it's all right," Arturo said. "They won't hurt me. I will not disappear." His large sad eyes turned to Mr. Clay.

Mr. Clay in turn spoke to the small crowd of friends.

"Ted, take this gang to the ice cream store. I'll take Arturo and Mrs. DeCosta to the police station. They know about the coercion." He winked at Polly. "They want justice as much as we do. There is nothing more you can do. Not tonight. If he is called to appear before the judge, then you can help. This shouldn't take long. Maybe we'll be able to join you later."

Polly blinked in surprise. Kyle the Clam's dad was going to defend Arturo.

"You never said your dad was a lawyer."

"You never asked. He teaches law at the university," Kyle whispered.

"Are you rich?" Rosalie asked.

"My folks believe in living simply. Something about the trap of middle class materialism, or debilitating effects of bourgeois patterns of affluence," Kyle said.

"Huh?" Rosalie and Polly both moaned.

"If we have money we don't spend it on more stuff for ourselves."

"Sounds serious," Polly grinned. "Let's go for ice cream. I need a hamburger and fries, too."

Her dad was helping Isabel on with her shawl. Mr. Jones was yakking to parents. Mrs. Clay had gone with her husband and the DeCostas. Rosalie had asked to stay with Polly.

"Let's go, folks," Polly's dad shouted. "Enough of this malipalaver. I've got to get over to the mall for Midnight Madness."

14. The Chase

POLLY'S DAD DROVE THE CAR AROUND TO THE EXIT closest to his store, Excelsports. Polly, Kyle, and Rosalie sat in the back seat. Isabel was in front.

"You guys will have to walk home. I have to stay to close the place down."

"Isn't that Thorn's van parked over by the Pancake House?" Kyle pointed. A police car sat beside the brown van. Rosalie shivered.

"It's okay, Rosalie. Probably the police have him by now," Polly said. She clutched her pack with her wallet and sketch book in it.

"Why don't you leave that in the car, honey?" her dad asked. Polly shook her head and hauled the knapsack with her as they walked to the ice cream store in the food fair. Fountains splashed. Christmas carols were being played by a string quartet dressed in white and black like penguins. They filled the busy promenade with happy sounds. The giant Christmas tree rotated on a stand in the centre of the mall. Even this late at night little kids were lined up to see Santa.

"Should be in bed," Isabel stated bluntly.

Jonesy was already at the store and had saved a row of tables in the non-smoking section.

"Sure good to have my old teacher as a neighbour," he laughed, clapping Isabel on the shoulder. "She taught me everything I know."

"Come on now, Howie," Isabel blushed. "I was just your supervisor for your practice teaching."

"Might even talk her into being a volunteer in the art room, in her spare time."

"Oh, Howie," Isabel said. "If a retired teacher...."

Kyle and Polly stared at each other. "Howie?" they muttered under their breath. "Jonesy's name is Howie?" They both snickered.

"Well, look who's coming?" Polly's dad pointed down the glittering row of stores. Walking their way were Detective Mills and the young guy, Connelly, who'd had his head in the garbage can at Thorn's and had rescued Polly and Robin.

Isabel called them over. "Why don't you join us? Bring us up to date on the investigation."

"You must be pretty pleased. Catching the gang leader like that." Polly's dad gestured wildly with his hands. "Name your poison, kids." He bounced to his feet, unrolling bills from his wallet.

Polly shook her head. What a dad. She blushed. He looked kind of silly, but then who didn't? She pulled out her sketch pad to draw him.

"Well, unfortunately, it seems we've lost Thorn," Detective Mills scowled. "We followed him and the girl the kids call Spiker here. They had no stolen property in the house that we can see and none in the van, so we wanted more evidence before we made the arrest."

"That's because Rudy took it all with him." Polly hit her head with the palm of her hand. "Didn't you chase him? He's gone to BC to deliver a car and dump the stolen goods."

Detective Mills came and sat down next to Polly. Polly flipped the pages of her sketchbook to the picture of the interior of Rudy's shop. "See, I figure all those boxes have the stolen Christmas presents, probably Weinsteins's jewellery ..." She glanced at Isabel, "...and Isabel's box of gems."

"Why didn't you tell us?" Detective Mills asked.

"I wasn't sure until I worked it out this afternoon. You were busy."

"I wasn't expecting you kids to keep following up on clues," the young woman said. "I didn't know kids were so persistent."

"Very determined pair," Isabel said. She dug into her banana split. "Not much patience with adults, though." She winked at Polly.

Oh, oh, thought Polly, that's true, that's true. She had blown up at her folks. They'd come to the concert, but were they really back to being friends? She touched the heliotrope. What she needed was to be more patient, especially if she was going to convince grownups she was not a little kid anymore. The Powerfully Patient Polly McDoodle wondered if there was a gem for patience.

"RUDY IS THORN'S UNCLE," Kyle said.

"We knew that. We just didn't know he was involved. He's been going straight for some time." Detective

Mills took the cone Polly's dad offered her. "Seems we missed quite a few things." She was flipping through Polly's sketch book.

"What's this?" She pointed to the picture of the Kims's backyard.

"They were burying something," Polly said.

"Probably their kimchee," the younger detective said. "If they are Korean – like one half of me is – they bury ten or twenty kilos of fermenting cabbage to make kimchee."

"Twenty kilos of cabbage!" Polly and Kyle made ugly faces at the thought of old cabbage.

"For a while we suspected the Twins."

"Growing marijuana and training little crooks," Polly added.

"No, they own a flower shop and grow rare tropical plants." Detective Mills smiled. "We checked them out."

Ted McDougall handed Kyle a double-dipped chocolate cone.

"How did you know Arturo was working for Thorn?" Detective Mills asked. Polly chewed the last of her hamburger, licked her fingers, and took her cone from her dad. Slowly, patiently, she explained things.

"He had a *Journal* bag and no route. He was afraid of Thorn. He got sick when he realized what he had done and that the rest of us were beginning to figure things out. He felt real bad, Detective Mills. He only did it because Thorn intimidated him. He's not a bad kid. Will he have to go to jail?" Polly patted Rosalie's hand. "He fed George cookies while Thorn ripped off Isabel's apartment. Then he put the loot in the back of the van.

Thorn never carried anything if he could help it. He patroled the neighbourhoods, checking on the apartments where he had kids working for him. They carried the stuff. Arturo gave you that picture of the elusive rabbit, didn't he? I left it on the counter by the phone in Isabel's."

Rosalie nodded, her black hair falling over her forehead. "You can have it back."

"You coloured it, you keep it," Polly asserted. "It was just another clue."

"Kyle found the telephone list in the tree," Isabel said. "That's how you figured out how the robberies were set up. The two of you also rescued poor George."

"George?" Detective Mills asked. "Who's George?"

Isabel explained about the dropped drugs and the drowsy dog. Everyone laughed at the description of the poor terrier with his wobbly legs and loud snores.

"You're quite the artist." Detective Mills continued studying Polly's sketches. "Who's this?"

"That's Thorn without his punk outfit." She turned back to the picture of Spiker at the kitchen window. "Here's Spiker without orange hair, giant earrings, or gobs of makeup."

"Can I have these?" Detective Mills stood quickly. "We followed them into the mall. They led us on a merry chase up and down and around until we lost them. We have officers watching on all levels. That's one of the disadvantages of giant malls. You can really disappear. These pictures will help."

"They won't go back to the van, that's for sure," Kyle said. "Arturo said they were going to make a break for it. He heard them when he took back the *Journal* bag and dropped it on the back porch."

"He ran away before we could talk to him," Detective Mills said. "They could still be in here."

"We've been looking for two punks," the younger detective said. "If they bought new clothes and went to a hair salon they'd look different."

Without a word Kyle and Polly sprang to their feet. Kyle motioned to the escalators. Isabel took Rosalie's hand. "You stay with me...in case your mama comes."

"Don't do anything foolish," Polly's dad waved. "I'll be in my store if you need me."

Both detectives followed the kids to the top floor, winding their way through crowds of shoppers carrying heavy parcels, wheeling carts or baby strollers.

Polly and Kyle knew where they were going. At the end of the first street to the left was a major hair salon.

Detective Mills caught up to them as they reached the counter.

"Have you waited on a guy with purple braids and a girl with orange spiky hair tonight?" Polly asked.

The tall fellow with beaded dreadlocks behind the desk nodded. "Funny thing, sweetie." Then he hesitated. "What's it to you?"

Detective Mills flashed her badge.

"Hey, Dorry, come tell this police officer about the converted punkers." A girl came from behind the purple baffle, wiping her hands on a monogrammed towel.

"Oh, yeah. Well, these two punkers, looking real cool, eh, they came in here in a panic around six o'clock, asking what it would take to make them look real straight, eh, like Sunday School teachers, 'cause the guy's dear grandma had died, and he had to go to the funeral. Couldn't go looking funky."

"It was a real challenge," the hairdresser said. "They had really ruined their hair, you know, with too much gel and mousse and not enough...."

"Never mind, Jeffery. The police aren't interested in that, eh?"

Detective Mills flashed the sketches of Thorn and Spiker in their before and after poses as drawn by Polly.

"Hey, you've got one of those police artists we hear about – what do you know." Dorry passed the book to Jeffery.

"Hey, man – I mean, hey, officer, that's them. You got it. Don't know if the clothes are right but they had bags of them from the department stores here in the mall."

"Too bad you didn't get here half an hour ago. You could have talked to them yourself." Dorry flipped her cascades of bleached blonde curls.

"They were in here that long?" Kyle asked.

"It takes a long time to get all the colour out," Dorry said. "And new in. It's a real art. After all, for someone's funeral I wanted them to look nice."

Detective Mills was talking on the walkie-talkie. She handed the sketch book to Connelly, the young detective. "Here, take this and make copies for the rest. Anderson is coming from the station with all the evidence we need from Arturo, the poor kid. Wait till I get my hands on Thorn."

Kyle and Polly stood watching it all.

"The only funeral Thorn's going to is his own," Polly chuckled.

"They don't hang criminals," Kyle said. "That's barbaric. But they'll put him away for a while, teach him some manners."

"You don't sound like any clam right now." Polly walked towards the escalator. "Let's go and tell Isabel and Rosalie."

"And Howie Jones," Kyle snorted. "Wait till the kids hear this. Howie Jones!"

Isabel and Jonesy were still sitting talking, sipping coffee.

"Any luck?" Isabel asked.

"Where's Rosalie?" Polly asked.

"Her mother came and took her home," Jonesy said. "Arturo has to be in court tomorrow at 9:30 a.m., so you kids better get home to bed, if you're planning on going to support him."

"I'll just run and say goodnight to my dad," Polly said.

Kyle padded along beside her not saying a word. Clowns cavorted on a stage in the next junction of mall streets. He hummed, "I'd like to teach the world to sing in perfect harmony."

"I'm tired." Polly slowed to look in the hobby store window at artist's supplies. The glass of the hobby store window reflected the scene in the mall as well as showing off the easel and paints. Polly could see Detective Anderson, tall and broad in his neat grey suit and suede shoes, sauntering along the other side of the mall street peering in store windows. She waved.

"If I was making a run for it, I'd go to the bank and buy plenty of food," Kyle mused. "Then steal a car from a busy mall parking lot."

"I wonder if they've checked Safeway?" Polly dashed down the corridor toward the giant food store with Kyle close behind her. Detective Anderson, spotting her and Kyle, hurried after them. They pushed past two of Santa's elves jingling in the middle of the hallway, a lumbering Root Beer Bear with free tickets, and a giggling group of teenagers dressed in black. The smell of cinnamon buns and fresh coffee filled their nostrils as they ran. Polly nearly tripped over a clerk who was handing out tiny cubes of Ukrainian sausage jammed on toothpicks. The ceiling light over the ice cream counter hissed and blinked on and off, shedding an eerie light on the marble floor. A pyramid of Christmas holly paper towels teetered as Polly and Kyle skirted it at the entrance to Safeway.

Polly stopped suddenly, breathing hard and lifted her hand. Kyle froze beside her. Their eyes flickered, squinting in the harsh fluorescent lights. They searched the store for signs of Thorn and Spiker. Detective Anderson came up behind them. "What's up?"

"Look!" Polly pointed at a sweet-looking young couple by the check-out, both with short blonde hair, the guy in a neat ski jacket and cords, the woman in a brand-new pastel pink winter jacket and white jeans. "There they are!"

"Are you sure?" Detective Anderson pushed past Polly and walked briskly towards the front of the store. The two blondes spotted him, picked up their groceries and ran for the exit. Detective Anderson pulled his walkie-talkie from his pocket and barked into it. Then he ran after them, waving the kids away. "Go home!"

POLLY'S MOTHER SAT at their kitchen table nursing a

cup of cocoa and nibbling shortbread. She was reading the information about Kirby and had a bus map propped in front of her. She glanced up as Polly tiptoed in.

"Your brother went out with the team for treats," she said. "So I came home. Alone." Polly's mom sighed. "One kid doesn't want me and the other feels left out. It's too much."

Polly, still exhilarated from the chase, couldn't miss the sadness in her mom's voice. She put on the kettle, got down a mug and some marshmallows and sat down. She breathed deeply.

"Kids grow up too fast," Mom said. "One day they're babies, the next thing you know they're out with their buddies or yelling at you. I don't adjust well to growing kids."

"I'm sorry I yelled."

"Don't make a habit of it."

"I won't."

The kettle whistled. Polly made her cocoa and raided the tin of peanut butter cookies. "Do you want another cup?" She waved the kettle at her mom.

Mom stacked the map and info sheets about schools neatly and put them on the counter. She handed Polly her empty mug. "You really love drawing...that much?"

Polly nodded.

"Those backdrops were impressive. Isabel says you have talent." She frowned at her hands. "If it doesn't work out, if you aren't good enough, you'll be hurt." Mom's voice was low. Polly sensed somehow that her mother was talking to herself as well as Polly. "You'll have to modify your dream. That's hard to do, let me tell you, that's hard to do. You find happiness anyway, but it takes time. Might be better not to dream so big."

Polly stirred her cocoa, let the rich foamy marshmallow spread across the top of the mug. Her mother was looking right into Polly's eyes, making some decision. Finally she spoke, her voice barely more than a whisper.

"I was one of the best young ballet dancers in the city. I loved it, Polly, just as much as you love drawing, maybe more. When they came to audition for the National Ballet School everyone thought I'd be chosen." Her mother paused, and cleared her throat and blinked several times. "The judges chose two other little girls. My parents asked them why I hadn't been accepted. The judges said my form was better and my sense of rhythm, but they could tell by my bone structure that I would be too big, too heavy to be carried." Mom's face was pink as if she had been running for blocks.

Polly stirred her hot chocolate. No wonder her mother didn't want her to get too serious about art. The vision of the iceberg floated across Polly's mind. Everyone, it seemed – parents included – had secrets like Isabel and her mom, sad patches in their lives. When they talked about them, the sadness from inside seemed to well up like blues, grays, and mist. Everyone had parts of themselves that were invisible. Digging at the mystery of the Christmas crooks had revealed a much deeper secret. One about life. In one way or another all human beings are invisible. We look at each other and know only what we see and not all the rest. The Invisible Polly McDoodle sighed.

"What if Shawn doesn't make it?"

"We talked it through with him. He knows your

father never made it to the big time. Neither did I. But he's willing to take the risk. You're a girl. I wanted to protect you."

Polly reached out her hand and took her mother's hand in hers. For a moment the raw edges of revealed life and thought kept the two of them silent.

Polly's mother turned back to reading the small print on the information sheet. "They don't take everyone who applies, it says here. They don't take everyone."

"I know!"

"You'd have to take two buses."

"I know."

"You'd have to be responsible for all your belongings. We can't be buying stuff all the time."

"I know." Polly took a long gulp of her cocoa.

"We'll have to talk to your dad."

"I know," Polly said, grinning ear to ear, because she knew already, she knew without a doubt, what the answer was going to be. "Merry Christmas, Mom."

15. A Carnelian for Christmas

IT WAS FRIDAY, THE DAY BEFORE CHRISTMAS AND ALL through the apartment – waking Polly thought – and all through the apartment the presents were safe in closets, under the tree, or, thinking of the painting for her parents, safe at Isabel's. A noisy chickadee chirped on the black branch by her window.

She could hear moaning, strange sounds coming from down the lane. Polly pulled on her green sweats and sneakers, leaving the laces undone, clutched her keys and tiptoed through the silent apartment. Everyone must be sleeping in after the big events of last night. Shawn's team had lost but he had gotten one goal and two assists. He'd been a star.

Polly touched the heliotrope. No matter what happened today, you, little rabbit, are going back to Isabel. It's been great having you, letting you bounce on my chest, feeling your smoothness, watching lights reflect from your surface, but you belong to Isabel. Maybe wearing you around my neck has helped. I know more about being me than I ever did. I know I can't be invisible, don't want to be invisible, but that everyone has parts of themselves that are invisible. When you get close to people you might see their hidden selves. If they tell you some of their story, like Isabel had.

She grabbed her lime-green ski jacket and carefully closed the door, snapping it shut and locking it too. It would take time to get over the feeling there were robbers around every corner.

Polly shivered as the cold wind blew across the back porch.

"You aren't wearing camouflage," Kyle's voice floated down from the ramshackle fort, startling Polly. Winter mornings are so cold and quiet every sound echoes and expands like giant icebergs crackling in the Arctic seas.

"Some clam you are this morning, chattering like a magpie, enough to wake the Beamishes and half the neighbourhood." Polly climbed the rope ladder and threw herself down on her crate.

She stomped her sneakers to warm her toes. Beneath her feet something clinked and fell. "What's that?"

Kyle dropped to his knees and reached his arm through the crack in the floor, the same crevice where his dice had fallen on Monday.

"Something cold and metal," he mumbled, stretching his fingers as far into the hole as they would go. "I got them."

Polly joined him on the floor, watched as he pulled his arm out of the crack.

"My keys! You found my keys," Polly cried.

"The crooks never had them."

"The crooks never used them," Polly sighed.

"So it never was your fault."

Polly pocketed the ice cold keys, walked to the railing, stared out, thinking. "Do you hear something groaning out there?" Kyle asked.

"I think it's Thorn's dog, Brutus."

"Poor pup, let's go visit him. Too bad dogs can't talk. George, Brutus, and Chief could tell the whole story."

The two of them made their way down the lane. The street lights went off, leaving the dull gray sky, hinting of snow, as the only source of light. The Kims's cat jumped on the garbage can, setting off a real clatter.

"Kimchee. Ugh," Polly said.

"Howie Jones," Kyle chuckled.

Rudy's garage was locked and padlocked, a chain wrapped around the door handles.

"Wonder if they caught him?" Polly asked.

Kyle shrugged and ran to where the lonesome springer spaniel was yipping, snorting, and hurling himself at the fence.

"Poor Brutus, he's knocked over his water bowl."

"His food dish is empty, too." Kyle lifted the latch and pushed his way into the yard. He dodged piles of dog poop. The dog collapsed at Kyle's feet in a writhing heap of tail-wags, chin-dribbles, and yelps.

"Thorn and Spiker may be crooks but they liked their dog." Polly patted Brutus and crooned to him. Meanwhile Kyle searched for an outside tap. He found it but no water came out.

"It's shut off. We have to get inside," he said. "Too bad they couldn't take him. He's a great dog but he would have been a dead giveaway."

Kyle sprang up the back steps two at a time and shook the doorknob, turning and twisting it. It opened, throwing him back in surprise.

"Imagine, crooks with a rotten lock," he giggled.

Brutus scooted by Kyle and headed for his inside water dish, lapping like crazy. Polly followed Kyle and rummaged under the sink for dry dog food.

The house was a mess. Discarded clothes, dirty dishes, magazines, and shoes littered the floor and every other surface. One corner of the living room was clean and cared for. A saggy couch had a crocheted poinsettia afghan draped over its shabby brown velvet back. A tiny plastic Christmas tree stood naked on top of the TV with a small box of Christmas balls of red and green sitting on the floor as if ready to be hung on its spindly branches.

"Even crooks keep Christmas," Kyle reflected.

Polly walked over to the coffee table against the wall in the tidy corner of the living room. Several bonsai trees in black enamel pots stood in a line on the table. Polly bent and touched the stones, the packed moss around the base of the miniature trees. "These could be years old, but the Japanese found a way of developing tiny trees from seedlings that in the forest would be giants. Next to rabbits I love trees. I'd sure love a bonsai but they're expensive." She knelt in front of the row of beautiful green trees, their branches bending and reaching.

"They need water." She rose to get some. The springer had hurled himself onto a blanket by the big easy chair. A pile of newspapers and boxes leaned against the chair. Kyle bent to move them away from the tired dog.

"Well, lookee here," he said, lifting something in his two hands, turning to show his find to Polly who was carefully watering the bonsais. She stopped and stared in unbelief.

"It's Isabel's box."

Sure enough, the old cedar box with the initials "I.A." was clasped firmly in Kyle's hands. He held it out to her.

"It's empty," he said sadly.

Polly put the watering can down on the floor and took the box from him, checking it for herself, the creamy satin liner, the empty little nests for gems.

She looked up into Kyle's pale eyes. "Too late. We're too late," she sighed.

Kyle dropped down beside her on the floor. The dog came and sat in front of them, drooping his jowls on Kyle's knee.

"I wonder if my folks would let me take care of this dog. Someone has to." He wrapped his arm around the dog who shuddered and sighed.

"I could take care of these." Polly went back to watering the bonsais, choking back a wave of sadness. She felt other people's sadness all the way into her bones. Maybe she drew pictures to help the hurts go away, to get rid of her impatience with grownups. She was afraid she'd forget how Isabel felt, or Arturo with the sad eyes, unless she drew their pictures. Sometimes she drew just because a scene asked for it, and other times it was because her head felt too crowded if she didn't.

"I couldn't sleep last night," Kyle muttered. "Kept thinking about Arturo."

Polly let the fresh water trickle slowly over the colourful rocks and mosses surrounding the base of each bonsai.

"I read one of my old kiddie books." Kyle hesitated, then went on. "It made me feel better."

Polly looked up.

"I read *The Velveteen Rabbit*. Remember the Velveteen Rabbit?" Kyle nattered on, talking quickly as if he had found his voice and was trying it out like wings on a baby bird. "Real isn't something you are made, it's a thing that happens to you. You become! That's what the old skin horse in the nursery said." Kyle took a big gulp of air. "That's what I feel like when someone listens to me, I feel real. If nobody listens to you, you forget how to talk."

Brutus was licking Kyle's face with his big, wet, pink tongue. Kyle giggled. Polly listened as Kyle talked...talking to her, talking to the dog, talking as if he would never stop.

Kyle wanted to be listened to. She wanted to be seen. Arturo wanted to feel at home, maybe, to feel safe.

Kyle shook his head. "Enough of this malipalaver. We've got to get ready for court." He rose.

Polly hurried with the watering. She'd have to come back in a couple of days and do it again, unless Spiker came home.

What beautiful little trees, like little gardens with those sparkling stones. Those sparkling stones. Bending close she saw a funny little eyelet of gold on one.

"Wait!" she cried. The stone she held was reddish yellow and cloudy – a carnelian for comfort is what Isabel had called it.

Without a word Kyle picked up a gorgeous green stone from the nearest bonsai, nestled at the root of a miniature willow. "Here's the jade."

Quickly Polly replaced the carnelian and the jade in Isabel's box. Searching carefully, she and Kyle picked through the heaped gravel and rocks, separating the gems. Finally all but one of the satin nests were filled.

"Oh, shooting matches," Polly groaned.

"Hey, dreamer!" Kyle hooted. "It's the heliotrope. You've got it around your neck." Kyle leaped to his feet so fast the dog woofed and ran to the back door.

"Can we get in trouble for taking stolen property from a thief's house?" Polly asked as they ran down the lane.

"What's all the commotion?" Isabel was walking to the garbage cans with a plastic sack and George teetering beside her. "He's waking up. Still snores like a steam engine."

"Oh, Isabel, Happy Christmas." Polly threw her arms around the older woman's neck, nearly throwing her off balance.

Kyle pulled the cedar box with the initials "I.A." on it out of the kangaroo pocket of his sweat shirt and thrust it in Isabel's outstretched hands.

"Merry Christmas!" he said loud and clear.

16. The Courtroom

By 9:30 A.M. THE CLAYS, THE McDOUGALLS, AND THE DeCostas were gathered in youth court, Courtroom 444.

Polly had her sketch book and the file folder with all the maps and drawings. Outside, the sky was flat and gray as a submarine. The promised snowstorm had not come. The air smelt like snow but none had fallen. The temperature hovered around zero.

Isabel slipped in beside the group, touched Polly's hand. "You better come and finish your parents' Christmas present this afternoon. It's Christmas Eve."

Polly nodded her head. What a week it had been! Hardly a normal Christmas. She glanced around the courtroom. Mr. Clay sat in the front. Arturo and his mother were in the third row. Rosalie nestled close to Polly, smiling up at her.

"Looks like a church," she said.

Indeed, the official courtroom had oak chairs, the judge's bench, the clerk's desk, and two oak tables for the Crown Prosecutor and the Defence Counsel.

Kyle, the once-upon-a-time Clam, talked quietly,

pointing everything out, telling Rosalie and Polly everything.

"I think if I talk a lot, Rosalie won't be so nervous," he whispered to Polly. "See the woman at the front at the clerk's table, Rosalie. She has a tape recorder. So do both the counsels."

Rosalie looked nervous, glancing at her mother and Arturo sitting three rows back from the metal fence that separated Mr. Clay and the other officers of the court from the ordinary people. She shivered.

"It's all right, Rosalie. Don't worry," Kyle said softly. "Dad says it's going to be fine. Arturo has been very cooperative with the police. His statement will help convict Thorn and Rudy."

"Besides, he was coerced by an adult," Polly added, patting Rosalie's hand.

"Stand when the judge comes in," Kyle instructed. "Don't talk, don't even whisper too loud. Thank goodness, Arturo is the first on the docket."

Other groups of people sat in the courtroom in clusters. Native, white, freckled, brown, black. It looked like a United Nations group. A police officer stood by each door.

"All rise. Court is now in session. Judge Ludvig Smitt presiding," a guy at the front called out in a loud voice. "Arturo Romero DeCosta. The charges are listed."

"Is this boy represented by counsel?"

"Adam Clay, counsel of record." Mr. Clay motioned to Arturo to come and stand beside him. "The boy's mother is present in the courtroom, Your Honour. We waive the reading of the charges."

"Does his mother understand the seriousness of the

charges?" the judge asked.

Arturo stood very still beside Mr. Clay. Polly heaved a big sigh and glanced at Kyle. "Dad's got a plan," he mouthed.

"Yes, your honour," Mr. Clay stated.

"How does your client plead?" the judge turned his eyes back to Arturo. Polly gulped. Arturo looked so small, standing with this serious bunch of grownups, the judge in his black robe, the lawyers in suits or dresses. Polly clutched the folder tightly. How she would like to bop Thorn on the head for picking on poor Arturo. Detectives Anderson and Mills came in the back door and slid into two seats.

"I plead not guilty, Your Honour." Arturo's small voice with its thick Latin American accent floated across the courtroom. All his supporters sat up straight, ready to back him up.

"I am entering a plea of not guilty on my client's behalf." Mr. Clay put his finger to his lips and shook his head in Arturo's direction. "His mother is prepared to take him home, Your Honour."

"Is she prepared to take responsibility for him? He is up on criminal charges."

"She understands that, Your Honour. Several neighbours have come forward to help the DeCostas. Arturo is twelve years old, has no criminal record, has a good school record, and is a registered landed immigrant." Then Mr. Clay added, "Arturo was coerced by adults."

"The court would suggest a trial date of January 30 at 10 a.m. in Room 444," the prosecuting attorney stated.

"You can go with your mother." The judge half grinned and Arturo walked back to his seat. The whole gang got up, bowed to the court and tiptoed from the room.

"Next case," the judge said, clearing his throat.

"What happened, Polly?" Rosalie asked as they headed down the escalator.

"I think everything is all right. He's released in his mother's care. And ours."

Kyle coughed. "Dad says the statement that Arturo gave the police about Thorn, Spiker, and Rudy will help. He talked on and on about some other way to do this, so Arturo wouldn't end up with a criminal record. I didn't get it all 'cause I fell asleep over my cocoa listening to Mom and Dad talk it over last night."

Polly turned and saw the two detectives. She waved. Mills and Anderson were standing talking to two people outside the courtroom. One had a camera slung over his shoulder, and the other was toting a black leather case on a shoulder strap. Detective Anderson pointed to Polly and Kyle on the escalator.

"Wait up, kids!" the woman with the tape recorder hollered.

Down in the foyer a group of carollers gathered under a giant tree that went up two stories. Piles of gifts for the Christmas Bureau were stacked beneath the tree.

Polly and her family, Kyle and his folks, stopped to listen and wait for the two police officers and the two people with them.

"I bet they are going to take your pictures. It's not every day that kids help solve a crime." Ted McDougall patted Polly on the back. She blushed.

Kyle was chewing his lip. "So much for being invisible, Polly. We never really wanted that anyway, did we?

We just wanted to be taken seriously."

Polly nodded. She smiled, thinking to herself, Kyle isn't a clam, and I'm not invisible. We'll have to find some other nicknames for ourselves now that we are real, like the Velveteen Rabbit. Polly stared at her reflection in the huge window. She threw back her shoulders and straightened her back. Funny, she looked taller. Or did she just feel taller?

"Tyler, why don't you take a few pictures? Then I'd like to take this whole group to the coffee shop for a muffin and get the whole story. You'll probably be the front page colour picture on Boxing Day. This is great family stuff."

"No pictures of Arturo, though, or use of his name until we get him cleared," Mr. Clay said, tucking Arturo behind his back in a grand gesture.

Polly thrust her sketch book into Detective Anderson's hand. "You might need this."

"We've got news for you," Detective Mills said.

"Good news," Detective Anderson grasped Polly's sketch book. "Not only do we have Thorn and Spiker in custody, the BC police stopped Rudy at the Coquihala tollgate. He had a trunk full of stolen goods, just like you said."

Detective Mills scratched her head. "I've sure gained a lot more respect for kids. You and Kyle make quite a pair. I never knew kids could be so determined, so responsible."

Polly blushed, and her ears turned red and hot.

"I'm going to suggest that Arturo be put in the Alternative Measures program," Detective Anderson said. "He would have to admit his guilt and do some community service, but he would end up without a criminal record."

Kyle's face broke into a grin. "That's what Dad was talking about last night when I fell asleep."

"Maybe the whole fort, all of us, could do some community service, together," Polly said. "Like keeping the pocket park safe for dogs like George."

"You sound like your mother," Kyle giggled, "organizing our lives for us."

Detective Anderson blinked his eyes. "We'll see, we'll see. It would be up to Arturo's probation officer or youth worker to decide." Then he made his way over to Mr. Clay to talk about Arturo's future.

Polly lined up for a picture with Kyle in front of the sparkling Christmas tree. She looked down at all the boxed and unboxed gifts. There, right before her eyes, was a white rabbit with brown, velvet-lined floppy ears, a plaid vest, and a bow tie. She picked it up and turned to face the camera. The flash went off.

Rosalie grinned at the stuffed animal. "Like your drawings, Polly. It's the elusive rabbit."

The fur on the rabbit was smooth, and his eyes were wide and round as marbles.

"That's a real cute picture...snap another, Tyler," the reporter said.

Polly's mom and dad stood side by side smiling at her, her dad with his arm around her mother. Detective Mills was holding the sketches of Thorn and Spiker up for the photographer to take a close-up. In her head flashes and pops and coloured lights ricochetted, as Polly got used to the excitement and confusion.

"Okay, kids, Polly and Kyle, tell us how you solved

the crime." The reporter grabbed the two of them and walked towards the coffee shop, the families following in a small parade.

"It all started with the heliotrope...." and Polly chattered on, telling the reporter the story. Kyle filled in the details. "You should have seen our outfits...." They made their way across the wide expanse of marble.

Behind the giant tree through the tinted blue sky-scraper windows, Polly watched huge flakes of snow tumbling over each other, hurrying to the ground where a thick coating of white covered everything. She hugged the rabbit in her arms tight, then gasped and turned to give it to the Detective. "Look at me – I walked off with one of the Christmas Bureau toys, just because it looked like my elusive rabbit."

"Your elusive rabbit, eh?" the reporter laughed. "Your mascot. You've been pretty elusive yourself – wearing camouflage, lurking in lanes, hiding in halls." The reporter jumped up and did a little dance. "Hey, officers, how about we let these kids take this big bunny home with them, as a souvenir of their escapade, a reward for solving the crime? My paper will replace the toy this afternoon. What do you say?"

The police officers shrugged their shoulders. Polly hugged the rabbit close to her heart and followed the reporter into the coffee shop. Elusive, she liked that – the Elusive Polly McDoodle. Over the crowd Isabel winked at her, reached to her neck and pulled out the heliotrope on the chain, waved it at Polly.

Polly waved.

Kyle, the former Clam, was explaining in detail about the maps and the codes to the reporter. Then he and his dad hurried towards the old green Volvo. The rest of the group went into the coffee shop. Polly hung back.

"Where are you going?" she hollered after Kyle.

"To save a dog."

"George is fine!" she shouted.

"Not George," Kyle grinned. "Dad's going to help me get Thorn's dog before the police take him off to the SPCA."

Polly hugged TC2 close to her chest and waved as Kyle and his dad drove away.

about the author

MARY WOODBURY is the bestselling author of two other Polly McDoodle mysteries – *The Intrepid Polly McDoodle* and *The Innocent Polly McDoodle* – as well as *Jess and the Runaway Grandpa*, shortlisted for the Silver Birch Award in Ontario and named an Outstanding Title of the Year for 1997 by the Canadian Children's Book Centre. Her other titles include *A Gift for Johnny Know-It-All, Where in the World is Jenny Parker?*, and *Brad's Universe*. She has also published a short fiction collection and a book of poetry for adults.

about the illustrator

AN HONOURS GRADUATE of the Ontario College of Art, Janet Wilson is a freelance illustrator. Her work has appeared in magazines, advertisements, books, and films. Janet most enjoys producing childrens' picture books, for which she has received international acclaim. Janet Wilson lives and works at home in Toronto with her husband and two sons.